Bay *of* Souls

BOOKS BY ROBERT STONE

A Hall of Mirrors

Dog Soldiers

A Flag for Sunrise

Children of Light

Outerbridge Reach

Bear and His Daughter: Stories

Damascus Gate

Bay of Souls

Bay *of* Souls

Robert Stone

HOUGHTON MIFFLIN COMPANY

BOSTON · NEW YORK

2003

For information about permission to reproduce selections
from this book, write to Permissions, Houghton Mifflin Company,
215 Park Avenue South, New York, New York 10003.

Visit our Web site: www.houghtonmifflinbooks.com.

Library of Congress Cataloging-in-Publication Data
Stone, Robert, date.
Bay of souls / Robert Stone.
p. cm.
ISBN 0-395-96349-4
I. Title.
PS3569.T6418B3 2003
813'.54—dc21   2002192171

Printed in the United States of America

Book design by Robert Overholtzer

QUM 10 9 8 7 6 5 4 3 2 1

Lines from "To Juan at the Winter Solstice" are from *Complete Poems*
by Robert Graves, edited by Beryl Graves and Dunstan Ward (Carcanet,
1995, 1996, 1999). Reprinted by permission of Carcanet Press Limited.

Much snow is falling, winds roar hollowly,
The owl hoots from the elder,
Fear in your heart cries to the loving-cup:
Sorrow to sorrow as the sparks fly upward.
The log groans and confesses:
There is one story and one story only.

— Robert Graves, "To Juan at the Winter Solstice"

1

"BY GAD, SIR," Michael Ahearn said to his son, Paul, "you present a distressing spectacle."

A few nights earlier they had watched *The Maltese Falcon* together. Paul, who had never seen it before, was delighted by his father's rendering of Sydney Greenstreet. Sometimes he would even try doing Greenstreet himself.

"By gad, sir!"

Paul's attempts at movie voices were not subtle but commanded inflections normally beyond the comic repertory of a twelve-year-old boy from a small town on the northern plains. His voice and manner were coming to resemble his father's.

The boy was lying in bed with a copy of *The Hobbit* open across his counterpane. This time he was not amused at Michael's old-movie impressions. He looked up with resentment, his beautiful long-lashed eyes angry. Michael easily met the reproach there. He took any opportunity to look at his son. There was something new every day, a dif-

ferent ray, an unexpected facet reflected in the aspects of
this creature enduring his twelvedness.

"I want to go, Dad," Paul said evenly, attempting to exercise his powers of persuasion to best effect.

He had been literally praying to go. Michael knew that
because he had been spying on Paul while the boy knelt beside the bed to say his evening prayers. He had lurked in the
hallway outside the boy's room, watching and listening to
his careful recitation of the Our Father and the Hail Mary
and the Gloria — rote prayers, courtesy of the Catholic
school to which the Ahearns, with misgivings, regularly
dispatched him. Michael and his wife had been raised in religion and they were warily trying it on again as parents.
Sending Paul to St. Emmerich's meant laughing away the
horror stories they liked to tell about their own religious
education in the hope of winning a few wholesome apparent certainties for the next generation.

"I was fourteen before my father took me hunting," Michael said. "I think that's the right age."

"You said kids do everything sooner."

"I didn't say I thought kids doing everything sooner was
a good idea."

"You don't even like to hunt," Paul said. "You don't believe in it."

"Really? And what makes us think that?"

"Well, I've heard you with Mom. You, like, agree with
her it's cruel and stuff."

"I don't agree with her. I understand her position. Anyway, if I didn't believe in it why should I take a tender runt
like you?"

Paul was immune to his father's goading. He went for
the substance.

"Because I really believe in it."

"Oh yes? You believe in whacking innocent creatures?"

"You know what?" Paul asked. "This was a Christian Ethics topic. Hunting was. And I was like pro — in favor. Because Genesis says 'dominion over beasts.' If you eat the meat it's OK. And we do."

"You don't."

"Yes I do," Paul said. "I eat venison kielbasa."

Michael loomed over him and with his left hand put out the lamp on the bed table.

"'Tis blasphemy to vent thy rage against a dumb brute," he informed Paul. He had been teaching *Moby-Dick* with his favorite assistant, a very pretty South Dakota girl named Phyllis Strom. "Now good night. I don't want you to read too late."

"Why? I'm not going anywhere."

"Maybe next year," Michael said.

"Sure, Dad," said Paul.

He left the bedroom door its customary inch ajar and went downstairs to the study where his wife was grading Chaucer papers.

"Did he beg and plead?" she asked, looking up.

"I don't think he's absolutely sure if he wants to go or not. He takes a pro-hunting position."

She laughed. Her son's eyes. "A what?"

"In Christian Ethics," Michael pronounced solemnly. "Dominion over the beasts. He argues from Genesis. Christian Ethics," he repeated when she looked at him blankly. "At school."

"Oh, that," she said. "Well, it doesn't say kill the poor beasts. Or does it? Maybe one of those teachers is a gun nut."

Kristin had been raised in a Lutheran family. Although religiously inclined, she was a practical person who worked at maintaining her critical distance from dogmatic instruction, especially of the Roman variety. She concurred in Paul's attendance at the Catholic school because, to her own rather conservative but independent thinking, the position of the Catholics of their college town had incorporated Luther's reforms. Many Sundays she went to Mass with them. At Christmas they went to both churches.

"It's him," Michael said. "It's his funny little mind."

Kristin frowned and put her finger to her lips.

"His funny little mind," Michael whispered, chastened. "He thought it up."

"He always sees you going. Not that you ever get much."

"I get birds. But deer season . . ."

"Right," she said.

The circle of unspoken thought she closed was that Michael used the pheasant season as an excuse to walk the autumn fields around their house. With the dog and a shotgun borrowed from a colleague he would set out over the frosted brown prairie, scrambling under wire where the land was not posted, past thinly frozen ponds and rutted pastures, making his way from one wooded hill to another. It was a pleasure to walk the short autumn days, each knoll bright with yellowed alder, red-brown ash and flaming maple. And if the dog startled a pheasant into a headlong, clucking sacrificial dash, he might have a shot. Or not. Then, if he brought a bird down, he would have to pluck it, trying to soften the skin by heating it on the stove without quite letting it cook, picking out the shot with tweezers. Kristin refused to do it. Michael disliked the job and did not much care for pheasant. But you had to eat them.

And in deer season, certain years, Michael would go out with a couple of friends from the university who were good shots and the kind of avid hunters he was not. He went for the canoe trip into the half-frozen swamp and the November woods under their first covering of snow. The silence there, in the deep woods they prowled, was broken by nothing but crows and stay-behind chanting sparrows and the occasional distant echo of firing. If they got lucky, there might be the call of an errant Canadian wolf at night. And there were the winter birds, grosbeaks, juncos, eagles gliding silent above the tree line. And the savor of a good whiskey around the potbellied stove of the cabin they used as field headquarters. Killing deer was not the object for him.

Kristin, though she had grown up on her family's farm, forever borrowing her male relations' jackets with pockets full of jerky, tobacco plugs and bright red shotgun shells, mildly disapproved of hunting. At first, she had objected to Michael's going. He was nearsighted, a daydreamer.

"You shouldn't carry a weapon if you don't intend to take a deer."

"I don't shoot seriously."

"But you shouldn't shoot at all. It's worse if you wound one."

"I hardly ever discharge the piece, Kristin."

But a man had to carry one, in the deep woods, in winter. It was sinister, suspicious to encounter someone in the forest without a gun. Farmers who welcomed hunters on their land in season looked fearfully on unarmed strollers, trespassing. And sometimes, if he was standing with the others and a band of deer came in view and everyone let go, he would take his shot with the rest of them. He had never claimed one.

From the living room next to Kristin's study, their black

Labrador gave up his place beside the fire and trotted over
for attention. Olaf had been Paul's Christmas puppy six
years before and served as Michael's shooting companion
every fall. Michael bent to scratch his neck.

Kristin put her papers aside.

"Christian ethics," she said, as though she were weighing their general usefulness. "I don't think Genesis likes
hunter-gatherers much. I think it favors the shepherds."

"I must look it up. You always learn something, right?
Reading Genesis."

Early the next morning, two of Michael's colleagues from
State came by in a Jeep Cherokee. Kristin served them coffee and handed out bagged sandwiches to take along.

Alvin Mahoney, a tall, balding historian with a rosy
drinker's face, presented Michael with his hunting piece.

"Remember this? Remington twelve-gauge?"

Michael jammed three deer slugs into the magazine and
pumped them forward to get the feel of the gun.

"You can put six in there," Mahoney reminded him.
"Only if you do — remember they're there."

"Yep." Michael lowered the shotgun, unloaded it and
stuffed the shells in his jacket pocket.

The third hunter was a sociologist named Norman
Cevic, whom students liked to think of as coming from
New York, though he was actually from Iron Falls, a tough
little smelter town on the lake not far away. Norman did
his best to affect a streetwise quality for the small-town
adolescents at the university. He was about the same age
as Mahoney, twenty years older than Michael, though he
seemed younger.

"Norm went out opening day," Mahoney said. "Straight
out of the shotgun. So to speak."

"Wasn't it a zoo out there?" Kristin asked. "I mean humanwise?"

"Not if you know the territory," Norman said. "I didn't see a soul."

"You took the canoe?" Michael asked.

"Sure." Norman Cevic had a gravelly voice that amused the students. "Had to use it to get in there. Didn't see a soul," he told them again.

No one said anything. Paul was lurking in the kitchen doorway in his bathrobe. Norman took a sip of coffee.

"Except," he said, "Hmongs. I saw some Hmongs in the distance. Probably walked all the way in there. No snow yet."

"They need the meat," Kristin said. "They live on it."

"Roots," Norman said. "Winter greens. Squirrel. Raccoon."

"How did you know they were Hmongs?" Paul asked from his half-concealment.

"Good question," Norman said. "Smart kid. We should take him hunting next year. Want to know how?"

Paul looked to his father, then nodded.

"How I knew they were Hmongs," Norman declared, as though it were the title of a lecture. He had been cradling a Mossberg thirty-thirty in one arm while he drank his coffee. Now he put the cup down and let the rifle slip through his fingers until he was holding it by the tip of the barrel just short of the end sight. "Because," he told Paul, "they carried their weapons by the end of the barrel. Sort of trailing the stock."

"Huh," said Alvin Mahoney.

"Which is how they carried them in Vietnam. And Hmongs are very numerous in Iron Falls. So," he said, addressing himself to young Paul, "when I see a man in deep woods carrying a rifle that way I presume he's a Hmong. Does that answer your question, my friend?"

"Yes sir," Paul said.

"Hmongs are a tribal people in Vietnam and Laos," Norman told Paul. "Do you know where Vietnam is? Do you know what happened there?"

Paul was silent for a moment and then said, "Yes. I think so. A little."

"Good," said Norman. "Then you know more than three quarters of our student body."

"Mr. Cevic was in Vietnam during the war," Kristin told her son. She turned to Norman, whom she rather admired. "How long was it that you spent there?"

"A year. All day, every day. And all night too."

Just before they left the telephone rang. From his wife's tone, Michael knew it was his teaching assistant, Phyllis Strom. Descended from prairie sodbusters, Kristin did not always trouble to enliven her voice when addressing strangers and people she disliked. She had a way of sounding very bleak indeed, and that was how she sounded then, impatiently accumulating Phyllis's information.

"Phyllis," she sternly announced. "Says she may not be able to monitor midterms on Thursday. Wonders if you'll be back?" There was an edge of unsympathetic mimicry.

Michael made a face. "Phyllis," he said. "Phyllis, fair and useless." In fact, he felt sorry for the kid. She was engagingly shy and frightened of Kristin.

"I told her you'd left," his wife told him. "She'll call back." The new and rigorously enforced regulations required chastity in student-faculty collaborations, but Kristin was not reassured. She imagined that her anxieties about Phyllis were a dark, close secret.

"Do I really have to come back for this?" Michael said as they went out to the car. "I'll call you from Ehrlich's tomorrow night after six."

They drove past dun farm fields, toward the huge wooded marshes that lined the Three Rivers where their narrow valleys conjoined. In about four and a half hours they passed Ehrlich's, a sprawling pseudo-Alpine *bierstube* and restaurant.

"I want to go on to the Hunter's," Michael said.

"The food's not as good," Mahoney said mildly.

"True," said Michael. "But Hunter's sells an Irish single malt called Willoughby's on their retail side. Only place they sell the stuff west of Minneapolis. And I want to buy a bottle for us to drink tonight."

"Ah," Mahoney said. "Sheer bliss."

On his tongue, the phrase could only be ironic, Michael thought. Bliss was unavailable to Mahoney. It was simply not there for him, though Michael was sure he'd like the Willoughby's well enough. But for me, Michael thought, bliss is still a possibility. He imagined himself as still capable of experiencing it, a few measures, a few seconds at a time. No need of fancy whiskey, the real thing. He felt certain of it.

"How's Kristin?" Norman asked Michael.

"How do you mean, Norm? You just talked to her."

"Has she seen Phyllis Strom this term?"

"Oh, come on," Michael said. "Think she's jealous of little Phyllis? Kris could swallow Phyllis Strom with a glass of water."

Norman laughed. "Let me level with you, buddy. I'm scared to death of Kristin. Fire and ice, man."

Mind your business, he thought. Cevic had appointed

himself sociologist to the north country. In fact, Michael thought, at home the ice might be almost imperceptibly thickening. Kristin had taken to rhapsodizing more and more about her father, upon whose forge her elegantly shaped, unbending angles had been hammered. The god in the iron mask, mediator of manhood and its measure. Still alive under the granite. A man might well dread his own shortcomings in that shadow.

"Smartest move I ever made," said Michael, "marrying that girl. Definitely sleep nights."

Perhaps, he thought, that had not been the best way to phrase it, for Cevic the curious and curiously minded.

The landscape grew more wooded as they approached Mahoney's cabin, where they planned to spend the night. Farm fields gave way to sunken meadows lined with bare oak and pine forest. Thirty miles along they came to the Hunter's Supper Club, a diner in blue aluminum and silver chrome. Incongruously attached to the diner, extending from it, was a building of treated pine logs with a varnished door of its own. At eye level on the door was the building's single window, a diamond-shaped spy hole, double-glazed and tinted green. A hand-painted sign the length of the roof read "Souvenirs Tagging Station."

They parked beside the half-dozen battered cars in the lot and walked across the sandy, resin-scalded ground and into the metal diner. There were banquettes and a counter and a heavy young waitress in a checkered dress and blue apron. The restaurant itself was empty except for two old farmers at the counter who shifted themselves arthritically to see who had come in. From the bar, which sounded more crowded, came jukebox music. Waylon Jennings's "Lowdown Freedom."

Their table looked out on the empty two-lane highway. Michael ordered coffee with his ham and eggs and got up to buy the whiskey at the adjoining bar.

The bar had eight or nine customers, half of them middle-aged men, burnt-up drunk, unhealthy looking and ill disposed. There were also two Indian youths with ponytails and druggy, glittery eyes. One had a round, apparently placid face. The other was lean and edgy, his features set in what at first appeared to be a smile but wasn't. Michael stood at the take-away counter, resolutely minding his own business. Then the barmaid, whom he had not seen at first, came out from some storage space behind the mirror and the stacked bottles and the pigs'-feet jars.

The barmaid looked only just old enough to serve liquor. She had dark hair and brilliant blue eyes evenly set. She was tall, wearing black cowgirl clothes, a rodeo shirt with little waves of white frosting and mother-of-pearl buttons. Her hair was thick and swept to one side at the back.

"Say," she said.

"Do you have Willoughby's today?"

"Could be we do," she said. "Like, what is it?"

Michael pondered other, different questions. Could he drive out every Friday and Saturday and have a Friday and Saturday kind of cowboy life with her? But not really. But could he? Would she like poetry with a joint, after sex? Not seriously. Idle speculation.

"It's whiskey," he told her. He thought he must sound impatient. "It's unblended Irish whiskey. You used to carry it."

"Unblended is good, right? Sounds good. What you want."

"Yes," Michael said. "It is. It's what I'm after."

"If it's good we mostly don't have it," she said.

And he was, as it were, stumped. No comeback. No zingers.

"Really?" he asked.

Someone behind, one of the young Indians it might have been, did him in falsetto imitation. "Really?" As though it were an outrageously affected, silly-ass question.

"But I can surely find out," she said.

When she turned away he saw that her black pants were as tight as they could be and cut to stirrup length like a real cowgirl's, and her boot heels scuffed but not worn down from walking. He also saw that where her hair was swept to the side at the back of her collar, what appeared to be the forked tongue of a tattooed snake rose from either side of the bone at the nape of her neck. A serpent, ascending her spine. Her skin was alabaster.

He heard voices from the back. An old man's voice raised in proprietary anger. When she came back she was carrying a bottle, inspecting it.

"What do you know?" she said. "Specialty of the house, huh? You Irish?"

Michael shrugged. "Back somewhere. How about you?"

"Me? I'm like everybody else around here."

"Is that right?"

"Megan," one of the smoldering drunks at the bar muttered, "get your butt over this way."

"George," Megan called sweetly, still addressing Michael, "would you not be a knee-walking piece of pigshit?"

She took her time selling him the Willoughby's. Worn menace rumbled down the bar. She put her hand to her ear. Hark, like a tragedienne in a Victorian melodrama.

"What did he say?" she asked Michael, displaying active, intelligent concern.

Michael shook his head. "Didn't hear him."

As he walked back to the diner section, he heard her boots on the wooden flooring behind the bar.

"Yes, Georgie, baby pie. How may I serve you today?"

Back in the restaurant, their table had been cleared.

"He ate your eggs," Norman said, indicating Alvin Mahoney.

"Naw, I didn't," Alvin said. "Norm did."

"Anyway," Norman said, "they were getting cold. You want something to take along?"

Michael showed them the sack with the whiskey.

"I'll just take this. I'm not hungry." When he tasted his untouched coffee, it was cold as well.

Beyond the Hunter's Supper Club, the big swamp took shape and snow was falling before they reached the cabin. They followed the dirt road to it, facing icy, wind-driven volleys that rattled against the windshield and fouled the wipers. As they were getting their bags out of the trunk, the snow's quality changed and softened, the flakes enlarged. A heavier silence settled on the woods.

As soon as it grew dark, Michael opened the Willoughby's. It was wonderfully smooth. Its texture seemed, at first, to impose on the blessedly warm room a familiar quietude. People said things they had said before, on other nights sheltering from other storms in past seasons. Norman Cevic groused about Vietnam. Alvin Mahoney talked about the single time he had brought his wife to the cabin.

"My then wife," he said. "She didn't much like it out here. Naw, not at all."

Michael turned to look at Alvin's worn, flushed country face with its faint mottled web of boozy angiomas. Then wife? Alvin was a widower. Where had he picked up this phrase to signal the louche sophistication of *la ronde?* Late wife, Alvin. Dead wife. Because Alma or Mildred or whatever her obviated name was had simply died on him. In what Michael had conceived of as his own sweet silent thought, he was surprised by the bitterness, his sudden, pointless, contemptuous anger.

He finished his glass. At Alvin's age, given their common vocabulary of features, their common weakness, he might come to look very much the same. But the anger kept swelling in his throat, beating time with his pulse, a vital sign.

"Well," Norman said, "all is forgiven now."

Michael, distracted by his own thoughts, had no idea what Cevic was talking about. What was forgiven? All? Forgiven whom?

In the morning they helped Alvin secure the cabin. His twelve-foot aluminum canoe was in a padlocked shed down the hill. Getting the canoe out, they found the padlock broken, but the burglars, in their laziness and inefficiency, had not managed to make off with the boat. One year they had found the bow full of hammered dents. Still working in darkness, they placed the canoe in its fittings atop the Jeep.

A blurred dawn was unveiling itself when they reached the stream that would take them into the islands of the swamp. There was still very little light. Black streaks crisscrossed the little patch of morning, the day's inklings. They loaded the canoe by flashlight. Glassy ice crackled under their boots at the shore's edge.

Michael took the aft paddle, steering, digging deep into the slow black stream. He kept the flashlight between the seat and his thigh so that its shaft beams would sweep the bank. Paddling up front, Norman also had a light.

"Nice easy stream," Alvin said. "I keep forgetting."

"It speeds up a lot toward the big river," Michael said. "There's a gorge."

"A minor gorge," Norman said.

"Yes," said Michael, "definitely minor."

"But it gets 'em," said Cevic. "Every spring they go. Half a dozen some years." He meant drowned fishermen.

Yards short of the landing, Michael picked up the flashlight, lost his gloved grip and sent it tumbling over the side. He swore.

They circled back, and riding the slight current got a look at the flashlight resting on the bottom, lighting the weedy marbled rocks seven, maybe eight feet below.

They circled again.

"How deep is it?" Alvin asked, and answered his own question. "Too deep."

"Too deep," Michael said. "My fault. Sorry."

"No problem," Norman said. "I've got one. And it's getting light."

By the time they offloaded, the day had composed itself around the skeletal woods, each branch bearing a coat of snow. They fanned out from the river, within sight of the glacial rock face that would be their rendezvous point. Each man carried a pack of provisions, a gun, a compass and a portable stand. Michael made for high ground, following a slope north of the rock. The snow was around four inches deep. He saw quite a few deer tracks, the little handprints of raccoons, the hip-hop brush patterns of rabbits. There were others, too, suggesting more exciting creatures, what might be fox, marten or wolverine.

He fixed his stand in the tallest tree among a cluster of oaks on sloping, rocky ground. The view was good, commanding a deer trail out of the pines above him that led toward the river. Now the animals would be prowling down from the high ground where they had passed the night, struggling only slightly in the new fallen layer, browsing for edibles. He waited. Invisible crows warned of his presence.

Then there commenced the curious passage into long silence, empty of event. Confronted by stillness without motion, a landscape of line and shadow that seemed outside time, he took in every feature of the shooting ground, every tree and snowy hummock. It was always a strange, suspended state. Notions thrived.

He watched, alert for the glimpse of streaked ivory horn, the muddy camouflage coat incredibly hard to define against the mix of white, the shades of brown tree trunks and waving dark evergreen. Braced for that flash of the flag. Every sound became the focus of his concentration. He got to know each tree, from the adjoining oak to the line of tall pines at the top of the rise.

Michael had come armed into the woods for the customary reason, to simplify life, to assume an ancient uncomplicated identity. But the thoughts that surfaced in his silence were not comforting. The image of himself, for instance, as an agent of providence. The fact that for every creature things waited.

He regretted coming out. Somehow he could not make the day turn out to be the one he had imagined and looked forward to. The decision about whether to shoot led straight back to the life he had left in town. To other questions: who he was, what he wanted. He sat with the safety off, tense, vigilant, unhappy, waiting for the deer. He considered the wind, although there was hardly any.

The empty time passed quickly, as such time, strangely,

often did. It was late in the darkening afternoon when he heard a voice. As soon as he heard it, he applied the safety on his shotgun.

The voice was a man's. At first Michael thought the man was singing. But as the voice grew closer, he realized that the slight musical quality there reflected pain. He came completely out of the long day's trance and prepared to get down and help. Then, the vocalist still approaching, he caught the anger, the quality in the voice that dominated all others, the rage of someone utterly beside himself. Presently the words came — obscenities, strung together without a breath, alternately bellowed and shrieked as though they were coming from someone walking with difficulty. It still seemed possible to Michael that someone was hurt.

He scanned the woods in front of him, then adjusted his position to take in the ground just over his shoulder. At that point, he saw the fool.

A man about fifty came out of the pine cover forty yards away, slightly up the slope. If Michael's stand had not been placed so high, he realized, the man might easily have seen him. But the man's attention was altogether focused on the buck he had brought down, a fine ten-pointer with a wide rack.

"Oh shit," he cried piteously, "oh goddam fucking shit cocksucker."

He was struggling with the odd wheelbarrow across which he had slung his prize deer. It was a thing full of seams and joins and springs. Though it appeared altogether large enough to contain the kill, it could not, and its inutility was the source of his sobs and curses and rage and despair. And as the unfortunate man shoved and hauled, pushed and pulled his burden, covering the ground by inches, the extent of his rage became apparent. To Michael, observing from the tree, it was terrifying.

And justified. Because against every snow-covered rock and log the wheels of the weird contraption locked. Its useless container spilled forth the corpse of the deer and its antlers caught on the brush. Each time, the hunter manhandled it back aboard, whereupon it fell out again the other way, and the crazy wheelbarrow tipped on its side, and the handle slid from his grasp and he screeched in impotent but blood-chilling fury. Some men were poets when they swore. But the hunter below was not a poet; he was humorless and venomous and mean.

On and on, tripping on boulders, slipping on the ice and falling on his ass, endlessly locked in a death grip with his victim as though he had single-handedly strangled the poor thing.

"Oh shit, oh goddam shit the fuck cocksucker."

And when he stopped to stand to one side and kick the contraption — and followed that by kicking the deer — Michael, hardly daring to stir lest he be seen, buried his face in his sleeve against the trunk to repress the laughter welling up in him.

But now the fool, following the deer trail in his one-man *danse macabre,* was coming under the sparse bare branches of Michael's very tree. Michael could see his eyes and they were terrible and his red face and the freezing spittle on his graying beard. The man was covered with blood. He was humiliated and armed. Michael prayed that he would not look up.

He held his breath and watched fascinated as the man and the deer and the wheelbarrow passed beneath him in fits and starts and howlings. If the hunter below was possessed of the violent paranoid's tortured intuition, of the faintest sense of being spied out in his ghastly mortification — if he tilted back his head far enough to wail at the sky — he would see the witness to his folly. High above him lurked a Day-Glo-painted watcher in a tree, his masked, delighted face warped in a fiendish grin. If he sees me, Michael thought suddenly, he will kill me. Michael slipped his shotgun's safety off and put his gloved finger at the trigger.

Iced by fear, Michael's hilarity was transformed into a rage of his own. Oh priceless, he thought. Bozo sits up late drinking Old Bohemian in his trailer. In between commercials for schools that will teach him to drive an eighteen-wheeler and make big money, or be a forest ranger and give people orders and live in the open air instead of cleaning shovels down at the guano mill, he sees an ad for this idiotic conveyance to haul killed deer out of the forest. No more jacklighting them off the interstate ramp or chain-sawing roadkill, hell no, he'll go into the forest like a macho male man with his nifty collapsible wheelbarrow. Folds up into twenty-five tiny parts so you can stick it in your back pocket like a roll-up measuring tape or wear it on your belt. It was shocking, he thought, the satisfaction you took in contemplating another man's disgrace. Another man's atoned for your own.

Finally, cursing and howling, the hunter bore his burden on. When he was gone, Michael realized he had been tracking the man down the barrel of his shotgun, every stumbling inch of the way. He shivered. It had got colder, no question. A wind had come up, whistling through the branches, rattling the icy leaves that still clung to them. When he looked at his watch, it was nearly four and time for the rendezvous. He tossed his pack, climbed from his tree and set out for the base of the granite rock where he had left the others.

Alvin Mahoney was already waiting, hunkering down out of the wind. He stood up when Michael approached.

"See anything?"

"No deer. I did have something to watch, though."

Norman Cevic came trudging up from the direction of the creek, his red-banded felt hat low over his eyes.

"So, I didn't hear any firing, fellas. Nothing to report?"

With all the suppressed energy of his long solitary day, Michael spun out the story of the sorry, angry man and his wonderful device.

"Didn't you hear the guy?" he asked his friends.

Norman said he had heard nothing but crows and wind in the trees.

"Poor bastard," Alvin said.

"You're lucky," Norman said. "Lucky he didn't look up and shoot you. A local. Probably needs the meat."

Michael wiped his lenses with a Kleenex. "You're breaking my heart."

"Revenge on the underclass," Norman said. "Nothing like it."

"Oh, come on," said Michael. "Don't be so fucking high-minded."

"We all enjoy it," Norman said. Then he said, "You know, more game wardens get killed in the line of duty than any other law-enforcement officer?"

For a while they talked about populism and guns and militiamen. They had fallen silent in the dimming light when Alvin put a delaying hand on Michael's arm. Everyone stopped where they stood. There were deer, four of them, an eight-point buck and three females. One of the females looked little older than a yearling. The deer were drinking from the icy river, upstream, upwind. The three men began to ease closer to the stream, where a bend would provide them a clear line of fire. The deer were something more than thirty-five yards away. Michael tried shuffling through the snow, which was topped with a thin frozen layer, just thick enough ice to sound underfoot. He stepped on a frozen stick. It cracked. One of the does looked up and in their direction, then returned to her drinking. Finally, they came to a point beyond the tree line and looked at one another.

The target of choice would be the big buck. If they were after meat, the does, even the youngest, were legal game. The buck was splashing his way to the edge of deep water. In a moment all four of the deer tensed in place, ears up. A doe bent her foreleg, ready to spring. There was no more time. Everyone raised his weapon. Michael, without a scope, found himself sighting the shoulder of the buck. It was a beautiful animal. Magical in the fading light. Things change, he thought. Everything changes. His finger was on the trigger. When the other men fired, he did not. He had no clear idea why. Maybe the experience of having a man in his sights that day.

The buck raised his head and took a step forward. His forelegs buckled, and he shifted his hindquarters so that somehow his hind legs might take up the weight being surrendered by his weakening body. Michael watched the creature's dying. It was always hard to watch their legs give way. You could feel it in your own. The pain and vertigo.

"If he falls in that stream," Norman said, "he'll float halfway to Sioux City."

But the animal staggered briefly toward the bank and toppled sidewise into the shallows. The does vanished without a sound.

"Did you take a shot?" Norman asked Michael. Michael shook his head.

Examining the kill, they found two shotgun wounds close to the animal's heart.

"Guess we both got him," Norman said.

"He's yours," said Alvin Mahoney. "You shot first."

Norman laughed. "No, man. We'll have the butcher divide him. Three ways."

Michael helped drag the dead deer by its antlers out of the water.

"Anybody want to mount that rack?" Norman asked.

"I don't think my wife would live with it," Michael told him.

"I wouldn't care to myself," Norman said. "Anyway, it's not trophy size."

They were only a short distance from the canoe, but it was dark by the time they had hauled the deer aboard. Paddling upriver, they came to the place where Michael had dropped his flashlight overboard. The beam was still soldiering on, illuminating the bottom of the stream.

They secured the buck to the hood of the Jeep and set out for the state highway. This time they did not stop at the Hunter's Supper Club but drove all the way to Ehrlich's to get the deer tagged. When they had finished the forms for Fish and Game, they went into the restaurant and sat down to dinner. Mahoney was the designated driver and abstained from drink. He would, Michael thought, make up for it at home. He and Norman had Scotch, but it was not nearly as good as the Willoughby's. Then they ordered a pitcher of beer.

The menu featured wurst, schnitzel, potato pancakes, noodles and dumplings. There were deer heads and antlers with brass plaques on the dark wood walls and scrolled mottos in gothic script. A polka was on the jukebox and the place was filled with hunters. At Ehrlich's many of the hunters had family members along. There were women and children, even babies. Happy couples danced. The entire place rejoiced in an atmosphere of good-hearted revelry.

"Boy, is this place ever different from the Hunter's," Michael said. "It's not just the food."

"Know why?" Norman asked.

"Different people," said Michael.

"Different folks," Norman said. "This is Prevost County. They're Germans here. They're peace-loving. Orderly. You gotta love 'em."

"Do you?"

"Sure. Whereas the Hunter's is in the fucking swamp. Harrison County. Irish, Scotch-Irish, French Canadian. They're poor and surly. They're over at the Hunter's getting nasty drunk and selling one another wolf tickets. While here, *hier ist fröhlich*."

He spread his arms and with a cold, false smile enacted a parody of gemütlichkeit.

"Maybe we belong over there," Alvin Mahoney said.

Michael and Norman looked at each other and laughed.

Norman raised his beer glass. "Here's looking at you, Alvin," he said.

Alvin laughed. He was nervous, drinkless. It might be safer driving, Michael thought, to let him have a belt.

Michael was aware of Norman watching him. "You didn't shoot today," Norman said.

Michael shrugged.

As they were waiting for the check, Norman said, "I

have to ask you something. Over at St. Emmerich's, what are they teaching my friend Paulie about abortion? Me, I don't think there's much wrong with the world that doesn't come from there being too many people."

Michael poured out the last of the beer.

"I'm sorry," Norman said. "You're the only person I know to ask."

For the second time Michael was annoyed with Norman. Of course, sociology was the man's job. And he had never been subtle or discreet. He had been to Vietnam. He owned the big questions.

"They don't talk about it," Michael said. "Not at that level." He put a paper napkin to a tiny puddle of foam on the table before him. "They talked about hunting the other day." What he said was not exactly true. Paul was being taught that life began at conception. The rest, of course, would follow. But Michael was not in the mood to defend the theses of St. Emmerich's Christian instruction. Embarrassed, he flushed and hid behind his beer. He felt besieged. As though they were trying to take something away from him. Something he was not even sure he possessed.

Because I believe, he thought. They know I believe. If I believe. But faith is not what you believe, he thought. Faith was something else.

A blond waitress with a pretty, wholesome smile came over to them but she did not have the check.

"Is one of you guys Michael Ahearn?" she asked.

"Me," Michael said.

"Sir, you got a phone call. Want to take it in the kitchen?"

He followed her across the room, resounding with polkas, laughter, the rattle of plates and foaming schooners. In the kitchen three generations of women, the oldest in her late sixties, the youngest a little older than his son, worked purposefully. The warm room smelled of vinegary marinades. His wife was on the phone.

"Michael," she said. Her voice was distant and, he thought, chill. It made him think of the woods. Or of the light shining at the bottom of the freezing stream. "Paul is not accounted for. He was at the gym and then I thought he was going to Jimmy Collings's. But he's not there. And his school books are here. And Olaf is missing." She paused. "It's snowing here."

He remembered the deer at the edge of the stream. Its life ebbing, legs giving way.

"I suppose I called for moral support," she said. "I'm afraid."

"Hang in," he told her.

He walked unseeing back through the noisy room. Alvin and Norman were paying the check. Michael went into his wallet, took out two twenties and threw them on the table.

"That's too much," Norman said.

"Kristin is worried about Paul. He's out late."

It was snowing on Ehrlich's parking lot when they got to the Jeep. Alvin checked the lines securing the carcass of the deer. Michael took a back seat.

"You know," Alvin said, "kids are always getting up to some caper and you get all hot and bothered and it's nothing."

It was the last thing anyone said on the ride home.

The snow came harder as they drove, slowing them down. Michael watched it fall. He thought of the man with the deer in his wheelbarrow. By gad, sir, you present a distressing spectacle. If he could make it up somehow. His thoughts had all been mean and low. What he did not want in his mind's eye now was his son's face, the face on which he so doted. But it was there after all and the boy under snow. Hang in.

"Did I pass out?" he asked them.

"You were sleeping," Norman said.

How could he sleep? He had slept but forgotten nothing. His boy had been there the whole time. Prayer. No. You did not pray for things. Prayers, like Franklin's key on a kite, attracted the lightning, burned out your mind and soul.

When, hours later, they drove into town there were dead deer hanging from the trees on everyone's lawn. The lawns were wide in that prairie town. They supported many trees, and almost every bare tree on almost every lawn in front of almost every house had a dead deer or even two, slung over the low boughs. There were bucks and does and fawns. All fair game, legal. There were too many deer.

A police car was blocking Michael's driveway. Norman parked the Jeep on the street, across the lawn from his front door. Everyone got out, and when they did the young town policeman, whom Michael knew, whose name was Vandervliet, climbed out of his cruiser.

"Sir," Vandervliet said, "they're not here. They're at MacIvor."

MacIvor was the tri-county hospital on the north edge of town.

Norman put a hand on his shoulder. Michael climbed into Vandervliet's Plymouth cruiser.

"What?" Michael asked the young cop. "Is my son alive?"

"Yessir. But he's suffering from exposure."

And it did not sound so good because as they both knew, the cold, at a certain point, was irreversible, and all the heat, the fire, the cocoa, hot-water bottles, sleeping bags, down jackets, quilts, whiskey, medicine, nothing could make a child stop trembling and his temperature rise.

"Your wife is injured, Professor. I mean she ain't injured bad but she fell down trying to carry the boy I guess and so she's admitted also over there at MacIvor."

"I see," Michael said.

"See, the boy was looking for the dog 'cause the dog was out in the snow."

On the way to the hospital, Michael said, "I think I'm going to shoot that dog."

"I would," said Vandervliet.

At MacIvor, they were waiting for him. There was a nurse whose husband ran the Seattle-inspired coffee shop in town and a young doctor from back east. They looked so agitated, he went numb with fear. The doctor introduced himself but Michael heard none of it.

"Paul's vital signs are low," the doctor said. "We're hoping he'll respond. Unfortunately he's not conscious, and we're concerned. We don't know how long he was outside in the storm."

Michael managed to speak. "His body temperature . . . ?"

"That's a cause of concern," the doctor said. "That will have to show improvement."

Michael did not look at him.

"We can treat this," the doctor said. "We see it here. There's hope."

"Thank you," Michael said. Above all, he did not want to see the boy. That fair vision and he kept repelling it. He was afraid to watch Paul die, though surely even in death he would be beautiful.

"We'd like you to talk to . . . to your wife," the doctor

said. "We're sure she has a fracture and she won't go to x-ray." He hesitated for a moment and went off down the corridor.

At MacIvor the passageways had the form of an X. As the doctor walked off down one bar of the pattern, Michael saw what appeared to be his wife at the end of the other. She was in a wheelchair. The nurse followed him as he walked toward her.

"She won't go to x-ray," the nurse complained. "Her leg's been splinted and she's had pain medication and we have a bed ready for her but she won't rest. She won't let the medication do its thing."

Kristin, huge-eyed and white as chalk, wheeled herself in their direction. But when Michael came up, the nurse in tow, she looked through him. There was an open Bible on her lap.

The nurse went to take the handles of Kristin's wheelchair. Michael stepped in and took them himself. Do its thing? He had trouble turning the wheelchair around. The rear wheels refused to straighten out. Do their thing. He pushed his wife toward the wall. Her splinted right leg extended straight out and when its foot touched the wall, she uttered a soft cry. Tears ran down her face.

"There's a little trick to it," said the nurse. She made a sound that was not quite a laugh. "Let me."

Michael ignored her. The wheelchair resisted his trembling pressure. Oh goddam shit.

"Take me in to him," Kristin said.

"Better not," the nurse said, to Michael's relief.

If he could see himself, futilely trying to ambulate his wife on wheels, Michael thought, it would be funny. But hospitals never had mirrors. There was a discovery. In the place of undoings, where things came apart, your children changed to cadavers, you spun your wife in wheelies, no mirrors. The joke was on you but you did not have to watch yourself.

When they were in the room she said, "I fell carrying him. He was by the garden fence — I fell in the snow." He could picture her carrying Paul up from the garden, tripping, slipping, stumbling. He took her icy hand but she withdrew it. "He was so cold."

"Lie down," he said. "Can you?"

"No, it hurts."

He stood and rang for the nurse.

Kristin took up the Bible as though she were entranced and began to read aloud.

"'Be merciful unto me, O God, be merciful unto me: for my soul trusteth in thee: yea, in the shadow of thy wings will I make my refuge.'"

Closing his eyes, he tried to hold on to the words. Listening to her read in her mother's strange featureless tone, he could imagine Luther's Bible the way her mother out on the plains must have heard it from her own parents. A psalm for fools in the snow. Really expecting nothing but cold and death in the shadow of those wings. Odin's raven.

"'Until these calamities be overpast, I will cry unto God most high.'"

Michael sat listening, despising the leaden resignation of his wife's prayer, its acceptance, surrender.

"'My soul is among lions,'" she read, "'and I lie even among them that are set on fire.'"

His impulse was flight. He sat there burning until the nurse came in. For some reason, she looked merry, confidential.

"I think we turned a corner," she said. "Michael! Kristin! I think we turned a corner."

Then the doctor entered quietly and they got Kristin into bed and she went under the medication. Even unconscious, her eyes were half open.

The doctor said you responded or you didn't, and Paul had responded. His temperature was going up. He was coming up. He would even get his fingers and toes back and his ethical little Christian brain going, it appeared. The doctor looked so relieved.

"You can have a minute while we get the gurney. We've gotta get her x-rayed pronto because she's got a broken leg there."

"You can see Paul," the nurse said. "He's sleeping. Real sleep now."

The doctor laughed. "It's very exhausting to half freeze to death."

"It would be," Michael said.

While they got the gurney, he looked into Kristin's half-open, tortured, long-lashed blue eyes and brushed the slightly graying black hair from them. With her long face and buck teeth she looked like the Christus on a Viking crucifix. Given her, he thought, given me, why didn't he die? Maybe he still will, Michael thought. The notion terrified him. He had stood up to make his escape when the orderlies came in to take Kristin away. Michael rubbed her cold hand.

The chapel was down at the end of the corridor. It had a kind of altar, stained-glass windows that opened on nothing, that were inlaid with clouds and doves and other fine inspirational things.

Michael had been afraid, for a while, that there was

something out there, at the beginning and end of consciousness. An alpha and an omega to things. He had believed it for years on and off. And that night, he had felt certain, the fire would be visited on him. His boy would be taken away and he would know, know absolutely, the power of the most high. Its horrible providence. Its mysteries, its hide-and-seek, and lessons, and redefined top-secret mercies to be understood through prayer and meditation. But only at really special moments of rhapsody and ecstasy and O, wondrous clarity. Behold now behemoth. Who can draw Leviathan? Et cetera.

But now his son's life was saved. And the great thing had come of nothing, of absolutely nothing, out of a kaleidoscope, out of a Cracker Jack box. Every day its own flower, to every day its own stink and savor. Good old random singularity and you could exercise a proper revulsion for life's rank overabundance and everybody could have their rights and be happy.

And he could be a serious person, a grownup at last, and not worry over things that educated people had not troubled themselves with practically for centuries. Free at last and it didn't mean a thing and it would all be over, some things sooner than later. His marriage, for one, sealed in faith like the Sepulchral stone. Vain now. No one watched over us. Or rather we watched over each other. That was providence, what a relief. He turned his back on the inspirations of the chapel and went out to watch his lovely son survive another day.

2

NIGHT AFTER NIGHT during the Christmas season, Michael burned until dawn. Neither he nor Kristin could quite regain equilibrium. He tried repeatedly through words and small gestures to provide some setting where the two of them might rest, take comfort and exchange the burden of their hearts. The sweet meeting he longed for, the mutual summoning of assurances and insights, somehow never took place. Lengthening her long jaw like a sword swallower, pursing her thin lips, Kristin absorbed her son's return from the dead as though it were her medicine. Pale and shivering, dull-eyed as a snake digesting a rat, she contained the whole awful business. It glowed through her, stretching her translucent skin like a frame.

During Christmas midnight Mass at St. Emmerich's, Michael sat numb and grieving, appalled at his son's intense, clear-eyed devotion. At the Kyrie he accidentally met Kristin's gaze. There were no questions for him there, no promises or confidences or happy conspiracies. Her look was as blank as the face of things themselves. It filled him with the terror of impending loss. He was the only child of a widow; his father had died in Michael's infancy. His mother had been erratic, demanding, flirtatious, constantly threatening him with the abridgment of love.

Kristin's mother had come for Christmas, on furlough from the nursing home to which she had retired after her husband's death. The farm, the fifty ragged acres left of it, had been sold off. Kristin and her mother spent the December afternoons examining old photo albums, doting over the pictures of Pop. Pop and a caught walleye. Pop on a horse. Pop in a canoe or behind the wheel of a new 1955 Buick. Pop with baby Paul. On the drive back to the nursing home, the old girl was vague but lucid. From time to time, Michael looked from the road to find himself fixed in her blue-eyed silent inquiry.

The trip home from his mother-in-law's required an overnight stop. Michael spent it in a cheerless river town that housed the state penitentiary. The prison's original building was a hundred-year-old fortress with crenelated towers and razor-topped walls, shrouded that night in river fog. At one guard tower someone had put up a lighted Christmas tree. Michael stood in the darkness outside his second-story room in the brick and cement motel — a structure itself like a cellblock — and smoked his first cigarette in ten years. But that was the last. He threw the pack away in the morning. There was Paul.

Nights were bad. He came to know the geography of night so well that he could tell the hour without looking at his watch. The stretch he knew best was between one and dawn. Light burned behind his eyes, resinous fires over which sparks whirled. In their glare his rage and dread brought forth bitter, unspeakable thoughts to be shaded, refined, reordered endlessly. Over and over the black insights appeared, one played on the last like tarot cards, spelling out the diminishing possibilities of life for him. Evenings he drank. And though he might sometimes pick up an early hour or two of sleep that way, the alcohol mainly served to keep him awake. He was aware of Kristin beside him and he knew that she was often sleepless too, often with pain, though her leg healed quickly. The bone had not separated and the cast was off by Christmas.

Still, he felt that some terrible misreading of the signs, some great incomprehensibility, was hardening between them. Every morning he got out of bed whipped.

A week after the winter term had opened, he went to his carrel in the university library to read. The campus was under deep snow, ice-crusted by weeks of boreal cold. Trudging up College Hill on a sunny January afternoon, he was blinded by the wind and the glare. The quiet world inside the double glass doors of Bride Library was warm and welcoming.

His small study was on the lower level, its thick-paned narrow window half submerged beneath the snow line outside. Only a pale winter light came, filtered through the needles of an adjoining pine grove. The fluorescent lamp in his cubicle was heartening and businesslike. Waves of heat shimmered against the lower windowpane.

The course he had designed for the spring semester consisted of works from early-twentieth-century vitalism — Frank Norris, Dreiser, Kate Chopin, James Branch Cabell. A hundred years late, his students were not entirely immune to its appeal. In the sterile ease of his afternoon's refuge, laboring under the same sadness he woke to each morning, he settled down with Cabell's *Jurgen*. It was a book he had liked very much as a youth, although recently he had seemed to run out of new things to say about it. After a weary page or two he went to sleep.

The exterior light was fading altogether when he heard a gentle rap at the door. It was Phyllis Strom.

"I'm really sorry to bother you here," Phyllis said. Her regrets were genuine because he had ordered her not to disturb him at the library. He stood blinking, running a hand through his hair.

"I couldn't get you on the telephone," Phyllis said. "But Mrs. Ahearn said you were probably here."

"She was correct." He directed Phyllis to the nearest library table, where there were two vacant chairs.

"I really am sorry," Phyllis said anxiously. "I know how you like to come here."

Michael laughed in spite of himself.

"Just goofing off, Phyllis. What's up?"

"Well, you know, I waited until the last minute to line up a thesis committee."

"Right," Michael said. It had been his fault. He had kept her busy through the break, shamelessly overworked her. She had never so much as breathed an impatient sigh. The rumor about beautiful Phyllis Strom, untrue so far as Michael could determine, was that as an undergraduate she had posed for a *Playboy* spread, "The Girls of the Big Ten." In any case, as a graduate student she had become a model of industry, modesty, sobriety and decorum.

"Well, you know I asked Professor Fischer when I asked you?"

Michael nodded.

"Well, I have a third person lined up." When Phyllis told

him the name he could not quite make it out. He had heard it around.

"Professor Purcell." She repeated it for him. "Marie-Claire Purcell. Everyone calls her Lara."

"She's a political scientist, and her specialty is the Third World," Phyllis explained. "She's real hard to get hold of on campus. Like she doesn't have e-mail and her phone's unlisted."

"Should I write to her?"

Phyllis blushed fetchingly.

"Your wife said you didn't have time to write until after term. So I wondered if you could catch her on campus today. I told her you might stop in."

Michael watched her for a moment.

"I guess I owe you, Phyllis. You were a lot of help to me this term."

"I feel so badly about pushing it," said the contrite but determined Phyllis Strom. "But it's so important to me."

"Is it? Is she so terrific?"

"Yes," Phyllis said simply, "she's great. She studied at the Sorbonne. She has a couple of books and she's been a television journalist."

"Wonderful." He had a vague sense of Mme. Purcell. One of the overpaid Eurotrash faculty who frequented each other's houses for edible food and adult conversation and liked to photograph roadside diners and picturesque gas stations. "Lucky us. Sure," he told Phyllis. "I'll call her. Is she in her office this afternoon?"

"Until four-thirty," Phyllis said with a guilty smile. "Please?"

And who could refuse Phyllis, wintry nymph with her tasseled elfin cap, frost-nipped little nose and principled ambition. So, in violation of the library rules, he dialed the college directory on his cell phone and eventually found himself in conversation with Dr. Lara Purcell.

"We probably met at the dean's drinks party," Dr. Purcell said. She had a pleasant voice, with an accent that continually surprised, with Britishisms and French words pronounced in English. It was not disagreeable. She was said to have grown up in the Windward Islands.

"Yes, probably," Michael said. They agreed to meet at her office in half an hour.

All over the campus, college groundsmen were salting walkways to keep traction underfoot for pedestrians, fighting a losing battle with the oncoming cold of night. The offices in the political science building were lighted as Ahearn jogged up the ornate steps, past the allegorical statues attending them.

The secretary had gone home but the department's door was open. He wandered in and found Professor Purcell at her desk. He knocked twice on her office door.

"Are you Michael Ahearn?" the woman asked him. She got to her feet and came out from behind her desk.

"Professor Purcell?"

She was only slightly shorter than Michael, who stood six feet. She was wearing an elegant purple turtleneck jersey with a small horn-shaped ornament on a gold chain around her neck. A short leather skirt, dark tights and boots.

"I've heard so much about you from Phyllis," Professor Purcell said. "You're her mentor and ideal."

"Well, bless her. She's a terrific kid."

"Is she?" asked Professor Purcell.

The wall behind the desk was decorated with paintings in bright tropical colors. There were photographs too, taken in palm-lined gardens with ornamental fountains and wrought-iron balconies. In the photographs Lara Purcell appeared with people of different racial types, all of whom shared a cool, confident air of sophistication. Almost everyone portrayed seemed attractive. The exception was a pink, overweight and unwholesome-looking man standing next to Professor Purcell herself. His features were distantly familiar to Michael — a politician, unsympathetic, one from the wrong side. But Michael had no time to study the office appointments closely.

"Well, I think so," Michael said.

"Call me Lara," Professor Purcell told him. She wore her dark hair shoulder length, streaked from the forehead with a shock of white. Her skin was very pale, her eyes nearly green, large, round and unsurprised. Beneath them were slightly swelling moons of unlined flesh, a certain puffiness that was inexplicably alluring. It somehow extended and sensualized the humor and intelligence of her look. Her mouth was provocative, her lips long and full.

Lara offered him a chair. "She's so serious, is Phyllis. And she thinks you make serious things seem funny."

"Who, me?"

The professor laughed agreeably. "Yes."

"Does she think that's good?" Michael inquired.

"I think she had her doubts. She didn't think it could be done. But now she sees the point of you."

The lady's cool impudence made him blink. It was not how people spoke to each other in Fort Salines.

"I'm glad to hear it. I'm very possessive about Phyllis."

"Rest assured you possess her, Mr. Ahearn."

"Please call me Michael. Phyllis," he said, "is very big on you too."

Lara only smiled. She looked at her watch.

"I usually stop for coffee at Beans about now. Like to join me?"

Michael's usual refreshment at the same hour was a glass of the whiskey he kept in his carrel. He decided the drink could wait.

It was tough going downhill on the icy pathway. From time to time one of them began to slide and had to be rescued with a hand from the other. Beans, the coffee shop that served the campus, was at the college end of Division Street, four blocks of thriving retail stores and service establishments that ended in the courthouse square. It was bright, its windows cheerfully frosted. The place was full of kids. At a table beside the door, some of the foreign graduate students and junior faculty were gathered at a long table speaking French. Entering with Michael, Lara stopped to chat. She did not introduce him.

They stood in line for their paper cups of cappuccino and carried them to a table at the back.

"I gather," Michael said, "you haven't agreed yet to serve on Phyllis's committee. And that I'm supposed to persuade you."

"She's sweet," said Lara. "She seems to have done her work. But I don't want any tears. I don't rubber-stamp the language requirement. And I expect a capable defense conducted in standard English."

"Phyllis is quite articulate. I can't speak for her fluency in French. She's intellectually curious. And of course she has a social conscience."

The professor looked over Michael's shoulder to throw a backhanded farewell to one of their colleagues.

"Her social conscience worries me," she said to Michael. "Please assure me. Will I hear pious prattle in American kiddie-speak? If I do, you see, she'll be out on her little bum."

Michael made a note to warn poor Phyllis of what awaited her.

"I'll vouch for her. I think we'll survive your scrutiny."

"On your head be it," Lara told him.

They looked at each other for a moment.

"You do hear a lot of silly uplift," he said. "Phyllis isn't that way."

"It's contemptible," she said with a fine sneer. "Life is a fairy tale and they're the good little fairies. The gallant little social egalitarian feminist fairies. It's our responsibility to keep them from getting loose in the world."

"Keep them down on the farm," Michael said, "before they've seen Paree."

"Right. Stifle them aborning. Because, you know, one sees them overseas," she said, "and one's ashamed to be an American."

"They can get nasty too," Michael said. He had somehow not thought of Lara as an American.

"But of course they're nasty. On their own ground, in absurd provincial backwaters of the academy — places like this — they run our lives."

They both laughed.

"You're blushing. I haven't offended you? Oh, but I suppose I have."

"No, you're absolutely right," he said. "Jargon and goodie-speak prevail here. Actually, I'm not sure it's better at . . . more prominent institutions."

"There are nuances," she said. "Places like Berkeley are exhausted by politics. They're in deep reaction, which is fine with me. At other places — Yale, for example — the powers that be are merely cynical."

"Tell me this," Michael said. "What's someone like you doing in an absurd provincial backwater?"

"It's what I deserve," she said. "And you?"

"I'm a genuine provincial. People like me provide authenticity."

"In fact," she said, "I planned to settle here with my ex-husband. The job was a great convenience."

"It's a nice town for kids."

She shook her head. "No kids." Then she said, "You'll want to be going. Your dinner will be waiting."

"Norman Rockwell," he said, "is stopping by tonight to sketch us."

A little flaring of the fine nostrils. "An artist, isn't he? A sentimental artist? So you think I picture your home life as a sentimental ideal?"

"Happy families are all alike," Michael said.

"What will you have for dinner?"

"We call it supper," Michael said. "We'll have pot roast."

"I mustn't keep you from it," Lara said. "You can tell your protégée Phyllis I'll serve on her committee. I hope she won't regret it."

"I'm confident she won't."

She offered him her hand. "And," she said, "we can get to know one another."

"Yes. Yes, I hope so."

Just before he turned away, she cocked her head and raised an eyebrow. As if to say it was fated. As if to say, inevitable now. When he hit the cold street, his heart soared.

It was a three-quarter-mile walk from the coffee shop to his house. The cold, the walk and the scintillations of his encounter with Marie-Claire Purcell had sharpened his desire for a drink. Kristin, in gym clothes, was in the kitchen preparing one of her quickie Viking specials, warm smoked salmon with dill and mustard sauce. She had taught two classes and spent the rest of the day at the pool. He went by her and took the Scotch bottle out of a cupboard.

"You're late," she said.

"I was detained."

"Really?"

He poured out half a water glass of whiskey and added water from the tap.

"By Phyllis?" Kristin asked.

"Sort of. You want a beer out of the fridge?"

"Sure," she said. "What did little Phyllis want?"

Michael got his wife the beer.

"Just wanted me to line up her thesis committee. So I did."

"Sometimes I wonder who's assisting who."

"Assisting *whom*."

She turned to him, put her beer down beside the smoked salmon and gave him the finger. Then she walked out of the room.

Michael quietly addressed the silence she had left behind her.

"Is there some rule," he asked, "by which every time I feel halfway human you get to throw a shit fit?"

He could feel himself coming down hard. It was downright physiological, he thought, the collapse of elan, the sensation of your chin hitting the floor. He kept the image of her retreating figure in his mind's eye, her upright posture, her waggling braid, her small perfect ass in the light gray flannel tights. Though he dreaded it, something about her anger aroused him.

He swallowed his drink. He was bored with pondering the etiology of his own hard-ons, his own insights, literary and otherwise. Bored with introspection. A man without a meaning was a paltry thing, and increasingly, since the day of the deer hunt, he had seen himself revealed as one.

Perhaps, he thought, it was not boredom but fear. They were closely related. Behind the bland irritation, the true horrors. His son came in, pulling off a hockey shirt and tossing it in the laundry pile.

"Mom's in a snit," the boy said.

"Have some respect," Michael said, pouring another drink, "for your mother's feelings."

"Huh?"

"How can we call the rage of Iphigenia a snit?" he asked. And while the poor kid was dutifully trying to remember who Iphigenia was, Michael commanded him to do the laundry. "Don't just toss that dirty shirt in there. Stick it all in the machine. I'll get dinner."

While Paul hauled the basket into the laundry room, Michael took his drink up to the master bedroom. His wife was not to be found.

"Kris?"

The door to the attic was slightly ajar but there was no light on in the stair that led up to it. He opened the door a little more, on darkness.

"Kris?" he called up.

"It's all right," she said. "I'm sorry."

He found the light switch and snapped it but the bulb must have been broken; the stairway and the attic stayed dark. He climbed the first two steps.

"You know," he said, "you must know there's nothing between me and Phyllis. I mean nothing."

"I believe you," she said. "I'll come down. I'll come down in a minute."

"I'm going to put your lovely salmon out."

"Yes," she said. "Yes, go ahead."

He stood in her darkness, wondering whether to put another foot on a higher stair.

"Go ahead," she said. "I'll be down."

Paul put the laundry through its wash cycles and Michael warmed the fish and finished making the tart sauce but there was no sign of Kristin. He put two plates on the kitchen table. By then he was well down the bottle of Scotch.

Paul, hungry from hockey practice, finished his first serving quickly and helped himself to another from the stove.

"Leave some for your mother."

"Of course, Dad."

Michael opened a beer to have with the smoked salmon. "You know what I think," he said to his son. "I think there's a vestigial reason why we like this kind of tart, rich stuff. Savory stuff."

"Like a prehistoric impulse or something?"

"That's right." He looked at the salmon in its yellow mustard sauce. "I think we used to like rotten meat. We must have cached it like bears. We're trying to get the taste back."

Michael paused and put his fork down.

"That's like so disgusting. Yarg. Cripes."

"You dismiss my thesis?"

Paul, who had enjoyed their banter since learning to talk, was discovering the difference between his father sober and his father drunk. He did not much care for the drunk game. He quietly cleared his place at table, emptied the rest of his second helping in the sink and prepared to do the dishes.

Michael spent another hour at the table, tapering off the drink, brooding haphazardly, recalling his meeting with

Lara. Then he remembered Kristin in the darkness upstairs.
When he went up, Paul was at his computer. The door to
the attic was firmly closed. Then he saw that Kristin had
gone to bed. Her braid undone, she lay facing the wall. He
went in and lay down beside her.

"I swear this to you," he said. "I swear it. There is no
woman in my life but you. No one. And if that is the trouble between us . . . then there is none."

She turned over to face him. "You wouldn't lie to me,
Michael?"

He put an arm around her.

"How can you think I would risk what we have for a little kid like Phyllis? She's a baby. I mean really, Kris."

Touching her cheek, he saw some question in the look
she fixed on him. It made him understand what it suddenly
seemed should have been obvious, that perhaps the trouble was not pretty Phyllis but something else, something
Kristin herself might not understand. The thought frightened him.

He got up and went to check on Paul, who had shut his
computer off and propped his Tolkien by the table lamp
and was saying his prayers. He quietly told the boy good
night.

"Night, Dad."

Careful of her wounded leg, he and Kristin gently made
love. It was great pleasure to have her long-boned, long-
legged body under his hands. A strong body, possessed of
surprising softnesses. She could be most avid, with a style
of alternate yielding and resistance. There was a kind of
physical pride to her; it was necessary to win her each time,
convince her. Sometimes it made him think of logic, little
syllogisms, discoveries, recognitions. But that night things

did not go very well. He kept imagining Lara; Kristin held back as though she knew his mind.

A few days later he had lunch at a burger joint in town with Norman Cevic.

"Miz Purcell," said Norman, "oh my!"

"So what's her story?"

"She had a husband originally. They were hired together. They'd been living in France. Teaching there."

"Her husband was French?"

"Her old man was French and he was considered quite a catch for the poly sci department. He was Ridenhour's kind of guy. But somehow she lost him along the way."

The late Dr. Nicholas Ridenhour had been a minor cold warrior of intensely right-wing views who maintained the university's political science department as a kind of woodsy clerico-fascist grand-dukedom. A wag had once declared that its members printed their own gold-based currency with Dr. Nick's picture on it.

"Lost him?"

"He got a better job back east. Solo."

"A practical man," Michael observed.

"Practical folks," said Cevic.

"So her views are like her husband's."

"Listen, man," Cevic said. "This is a dangerous woman. Really!"

"Dangerous?"

"Very smart girl this is. She has a following — a cultlike following — among some of the kids."

"She's attractive," Michael said.

"She's not attractive. She's about the hottest babe in the history of the state."

"She looks crazy," Michael said. It had not occurred to him before.

"She is. And she makes other people crazy."

"Phyllis Strom wants her on her thesis committee."

"Well, man," Norman said, "this is a struggle for a young mind. See if you can keep her from biting Phyllis on the throat."

That afternoon he suffered a breakdown in communication with his second class, an expository writing workshop. Led by an extroverted young woman athlete, the group undertook to address the personal problems of the characters in one four-page fictional narrative. The personal needs and available life choices of these thin conceits were examined as though they were guests on the kind of television talk show whose participants murdered each other.

"For Christ's sake," Michael told them. "You're supposed to be replicating life here. This is like a drawing class — the characters aren't real until you make them real. It's not group therapy or social work or an uplift pep rally! How about a little more literary criticism and a little less mutual support?"

The class sullenly dispersed ahead of schedule. He had failed to make himself clear. They had understood only that their youthful goodwill was being insulted. He had used abusive language. He had employed sarcasm. He had better watch it.

Rattled, he went over to the pool for a swim. The steamy showers and liquefactious echoes were comforting on that raw winter day. He had the luxury of a lane to himself. He swam hard, trying to outrun the shadow inside him. Some kind of bill had come up for payment.

He had, it seemed to him, done quite well by randomness. By the day at least, unless one insisted on pondering it all, randomness was no less cruel than some unlikely mysterious providence. He had always considered himself a lucky man.

Buying himself a cold can of grapefruit juice from a machine in the lobby, he came upon Lara Purcell sipping bottled water beside it. She was wearing a black sleeveless leotard and there was a damp towel around her neck.

"Doing your aerobics?" Michael asked.

"Squash."

"Where do you find opponents?"

"Oh, there are some formidable women around. I play men too." She drained her plastic bottle and tossed it in the receptacle against the near wall, a rimless shot. "Do you play?"

"What I play is racquetball."

"Oh," Lara said. "I can play that."

"Want to play tomorrow?"

"What time?"

"Three?"

But three might bring him home suspiciously late, if they stopped for coffee. It would be dark by four. They agreed to play at two.

"If you're good enough," Dr. Purcell said, "I'll teach you squash."

Back at his office he called Norman Cevic.

"So Lara Purcell," he told Norman, "invited me to play squash."

There was a brief silence on the line. "So what can I tell you, Michael?"

"Is that a pass?"

"Gamboling half clothed in a sealed chamber? What do you think?"

"I should say no way," Michael said. "I should decline."

"Did you?"

"I accepted. Racquetball, actually."

"You know," Norman said, "some of our colleagues — I won't mention names — are real screwballs. Disasters in search of a victim. Who knows what games are being played out? I'm not talking about squash."

"I'll call her," Michael said. "I'll make an excuse."

"Well," Norman said, "you're a man of the world."

Very funny, Michael thought. But it was not so. He was a tank-town schoolmarm's son, the grandson of farmhands on four quarterings, married out of high school. An over-educated hick.

That night the PBS station presented a particularly absorbing documentary about convicted murderers awaiting execution on death row. It left the Ahearns in mild shock. What terror to fall into the hands of a system so cruel and arbitrary as the law, so surreal in its unconcern for any kind of responsibility. It was the kind of thing that made you want to pray.

Kristin had not allowed Paul to watch because of the warning about graphic depictions. Michael, who would have preferred his son to see it, did not argue. Later he regretted it.

In the morning, he read the class papers on Kate Chopin's *The Awakening*. Many students had not troubled to finish the reading. Several of these compared it to *Madame Bovary*, which was presumably the posted line on it in Cliffs Notes or somewhere. A few apologized for their inability to sympathize with the heroine, vaguely aware that sympathy was the attitude expected. The class feminists abandoned Edna as a flibbertigibbet. Eros and Thanatos were too quaint and reactionary, even embraced in a solitary act of personal liberation.

It was hardly a surprising response. Solitary acts of personal liberation were what everyone must be spared or forbidden. They represented the failure of everything progressive. The courage to be yourself, a virtue much celebrated on campuses like theirs, lost its luster if you were selfish and boy-crazy and a bad mother, the way Edna was.

It occurred to him that he had been preaching against literary vitalism all his career, mocking the pretensions of the antinomians, the self-conscious libertines. If what he thought and said mattered, he would have to reexamine everything now. By midmorning he was beginning to associate the insidiousness of literary vitalism with his afternoon game of racquetball. He skipped lunch and went over to the gym in plenty of time. Lara had reserved the court.

They played for an hour. Professor Purcell wore latex shorts and a red club vest, her dark hair bound in a ponytail with black and yellow ribbon. She played facing the front wall, utterly focused, it seemed, on the game. She was fast and strong, not afraid of getting hit, not afraid of the ball. In two of their fifteen-point matches she beat him, and her game seemed to improve as they played. Their last game was the hardest for him; they exchanged advantage nearly a dozen times before he won it. It seemed to him he had never played a better woman athlete. When they finished the last game he had a quick vision of summer, of tennis and lemonade, a strange, happy anticipation of the sort he had not experienced for weeks.

Surrendering to his final victory, she took her protective
glasses off and wiped the sweat from her forehead and
rested her right hand on his shoulder. He was intensely
aware of her touch.

"Oh," she said, "you're good."

Michael had barely the breath to answer her.

"Will you teach me squash?"

She laughed and shook her head.

They met, dressed, in the lobby, lined with its trophy
cases and framed photographs of teams going back to the
twenties.

"Coffee?" Michael asked.

She hesitated. "Honestly," she said, "I'm well and truly
beat. You don't do massage, do you?"

There was no way in which this could be other than a
joke.

"I'm afraid not."

"Well, there's a Latvian lady I go to. I think I feel the
need of her."

"Good idea," Michael said. "If I had a Latvian lady I'd
go too."

"Oh," Lara said, "no, I feel selfish. Let's do something
we can both do. What you like best."

"I think my favorite thing would be to drink a beer."

"Decadent, eh?"

"Not at all," Michael said. "Wholesome. Agreeably provincial."

They drove her Saab to a sports bar in a mall surrounded
by dairy farms, whose silos and storage tanks loomed over
the fake tiles and tin towers of the mall. A few students from campus and a tableful of off-duty FedEx drivers were half watching a British soccer game on the bar's

giant screen. Sunderland against Manchester United. The screen commentary competed with Billy Joel.

Lara was wearing an ankle-length fox coat. Hanging it for her, he could feel the warmth of her body against the coat's silk lining. He ran his fingers over the fur. The bar sold draft Harp lager by the pint.

"I'll sleep tonight," Lara said with feline satisfaction. "I'm sure of that."

"I hope I do."

"Have trouble sleeping?"

He nodded and shrugged.

"Get the health service to give you something."

"Not my guy."

"Nonsense. Insist."

"Come on, you know how they are. He believes in valerian root. He believes fatigue makes the best pillow. He thinks people don't need sleep. He likes saying no."

"You should sleep," she said. "I'll give you something."

Her lips were inches away, and when he kissed her he thought he heard a little yahoo chorus rise from the bar. They sank back against the banquette. Michael was weak-kneed and dizzy.

"Want to play tomorrow?" she asked. "I'll teach you squash."

"I don't like all this losing-to-a-girl stuff," Michael said. "It's against religion."

"I'm a good teacher. I'll have you beating me. We'll turn it into an opera."

"Squash?" Michael asked.

"Squash is fate's game. The ball game. You have to be ready to die. You have to know how to sing."

"Maybe I can beat you," Michael said. "I get your clothes if I do. Isn't that right? I'll settle for that."

"Nicey, nicey," she said. "I'll have you singing in chains. I'll have your soft heart on a dish."

He kissed her again.

That night when Paul had gone to bed, Kristin asked him, "Did you ever think of joining AA?"

"Not for the merest instant," Michael said.

"I think I might join Al-Anon."

"Really? Getting bored nights? It's supposed to be a hot pickup spot."

As usual, she left the sarcasm lying where it fell, immune. "I've been thinking about how out of contact you are sometimes. As though you're not there."

They were on the second floor, tidying a spare room full of shelves they'd placed to accommodate an overflow of books.

"But I *am* there, Kris." Dumb denial was the best he could do.

She picked up an unjacketed book and looked at the spine. "I may be a dumb squarehead, fella, but I know when you're with me and when you're not."

They went to bed. Michael turned out his bedside lamp and turned over, facing away from Kristin. She lay beside him stiff as starched laundry, reading or pretending to read. He fell asleep before she did.

3

H E MADE a racquetball date with Lara for the next day and served ace after ace. Time and again their bodies touched, so that their match was compounded for him of brief sensory impressions, each one leading him to anticipate the next: her breast against his arm, her wrist linked for a moment with his when she retrieved his racquet.

"Call it yours," she said.

"No, yours."

In the shower he was inflamed, frightened and guilty. That morning he and Kristin had enjoyed a laugh together over the paper. Some droll, forgettable bit of buffoonery in an editorial. Their shared jokes had become infrequent; it had been heartening, a good omen. But no scalding water could wash away the shimmer of Lara's touch.

"C'mon out," she said when they were showered and dressed. "Let's go."

The assumption was that it was her house they were going out to. He climbed into her Saab. On the way, he ran his palm over the leather armrest. His eyes were on the warm turns of her thigh against the seat beside him. For God's sake, he thought, for once in your life, know the difference between what it is you want and what you don't. It had not been long ago since he had been reflecting on his capacity for happiness. Of course that had all been desperation.

"What other sports do you like?" she asked him.

"I like to swim. Every summer I dive wrecks up on Lake Superior. We've been through the *Virginia Giles* stem to stern."

"Really. I dive as well. Have you ever been in tropical water?"

"Once. On a charter to Bonaire."

"Like it?"

He shrugged. "There are no words for it. It's sublime. But the sunken vessels are what I really like. I went through the length of a German submarine off Block Island. I'll never forget it."

"I prefer coral reefs," she said. "Too many ghosts in wrecks."

It was a clear, nearly windless day. She parked beside the barn. He followed her and watched while she unbarred the doors. It was a six-stall horse barn and two of the stalls were occupied, one by a handsome chestnut, the other by a gray. Both of the horses had plain faded blankets. They turned at her touch, the gray snapping at her fingers until she withdrew her hand. The horse's breath vaporized in the freezing barn.

"Do you tend them yourself?"

"Mainly, but there's no shortage of farm girls at school if I need help."

She took a brush from a peg and began to brush down the chestnut's coat. This time she had troubled only to throw a ski jacket over the spandex workout gear she had played in.

"I exercise them in the morning. Are you an early riser? Come on out and watch."

"In the morning I'm feeding my own small animals sugar crunchies."

"Of course," she said. She walked into the next stall and brushed down the second horse. Then she hung up the brush and led him out of the barn and over to the main house.

"Want a fire? The makings are there."

While he was crumpling pages of *L'Express* and gathering shavings, she said, "I'll make one in the bedroom too."

He lit the kindling. On the living room wall, over a sideboard, the senator's picture was in place. In the next room, Lara sang to herself in French, a simple, familiar tune he had heard before. Perhaps a children's song.

He brushed the wood shavings off his hands and went into the bedroom, where she stood beside the stove and put his hands under her ski jacket and pulled him against her. She closed her eyes, smiling slightly. The feel of her body took his strength away gram by gram. The tan and white column of her throat, her strong firm breasts, the curve and cleft at the warm silky seat of that spandex under his palms' caress — blindness, vertigo. Mounds of earth, vault of sky, purity, corruption, incorruption. Heaven, the grave. Flesh as violation, bliss, freedom, offal, oblivion. Bury himself in her and fly, turn her into his own will. Her hair was damp and fragrant. It was all certainly what he wanted. Had wanted for so long.

Everywhere he touched her inflamed him; he shivered in the heat. She disengaged his hands and held them at his sides; he was looking into her strange aloof smile. Then she bent his wrists behind him, like a prisoner, and stood on his feet so that she was an inch or so taller. She kissed him on the mouth. Releasing his hands, she ran hers over him, pushing her thumbs in his armpits, fondling his erection.

"My dear," he said. It was an absurd thing to say, and quite properly she laughed at him.

In bed, she laughed at him again when he asked her if she had come.

"Several times, *cheri*. Yes, yes really," she insisted as though he doubted her. "Only tell me this," and she giggled softly. "This wife of yours, the Chaucerian, didn't she tell you where her clit is? Because" — she led his hand to the top of her vagina and brought his fingers to the button — "because it's here. *Voilà*, eh?"

Michael felt a rush of humiliation for himself, for Kristin, whom he loved.

"Or maybe she doesn't know, eh? This good and faithful one. When Mr. Norman Rockwell comes in the evening to paint you, ask him to show her where it is."

"I don't like it," he said, "when you demean people I love. I don't mind your putting me down. I know I'm an idiot."

"Ah, ah," said Lara, "I've been a bad person. I've insulted virtue, eh, which I wouldn't know if it hit me in the ass. So," she said, "punish me."

He saw that she was holding a strap like a dog's collar in her hand. She had taken it from under the pillow or somewhere about the bed.

"Go ahead. Punish me."

It was an odd little instrument, the strap. It had no buckle and apparently no holes to insert a metal tongue. Lara handed him the thing and threw her head back on the bed so that her throat was rampant, her forehead bent back. She showed him the whites of her eyes and stretched her limbs out toward the four corners of the bed, turning her arms upside down at the elbow.

"I've been bad, eh. I've insulted your little half-a-virgin of a wife." She put the strap around her own throat. "Go ahead, all-American boy, punish me."

He looked at the beautifully muscled structure of her throat, its strength, its perfect skin, and twisted the strap around it.

She looked him in the eye and cursed him in a French of which he understood not a word, and he twisted the strap until she had to stop. Then he held it tight against her throat a few moments longer. Her eyes widened. All the while she held her four limbs drawn stiff toward the edges of the bed.

There were red welts in the beautiful columns of her throat when he tossed the strap aside. She touched them with her fingers.

"Like it?" she asked.

He liked it. This time he had no trouble with her clitoris and they licked each other as if they were trying to dry off, thirsty, like dogs.

They lay in silence a long time after.

"Oh, God, baby," she said.

It had got dark outside. It was dark in the room, except for the light of the fire she had made.

"Oh, God, baby is right," Michael said.

"It's late. You're late."

"Fuck late."

She sat up and slapped his shoulder.

"Oh no! Don't be a child on me now."

"No? I can't be a child on you?"

"No. Uh-uh. You go and wash and go home to dinner and Mr. Rockwell." She moved across the bed and sat beside him and took his face in her hands and kissed him. "Or I'll have to send you away and you'll never come back and that will be that. Get me?" She nudged him hard in the ribs. "Get me, pal. Eh?"

"That hurts."

"Ooh," she cooed in mock solicitude, "poor *bébé*. Tough shit."

He went into her bathroom, preparing for his shower. Could he have lived without what had just happened? Done without her? The answer was yes, he could have done without her fine. He might so easily, now in retrospect, have been a person of principle and never let it happen. Too late now. He stood under the force of the water. Washing, washing, washing all day long. Baptized into pleasure, he thought. Free again.

She drove him back to campus to pick up his car. All the drive home, he pictured Kristin's suspicion and anger at his being late. It was nearly eight, too late for supper with the others, too late to help Paul with his homework.

When he had parked the car, the first thing he saw was Paul's vaguely worried face at the kitchen window. It had started to snow. When he went inside to the lingering savor of the night's meal, he realized how fiercely hungry he was.

"I put a few slices of lamb in the lower section of the oven," Kristin said when she walked in. "They'll be pretty dried out."

"I'm sorry," he said. "I got involved in the Phyllis Strom committee." The academic career of Phyllis Strom had its thorny aspect as an alibi.

"Really?" Kristin asked. "How's life on the Phyllis Strom committee?"

"Never a dull moment," Michael told her.

4

In the snow-sealed silence of his carrel, Michael read the reflections of one Keith Michneicki on Stephen Crane's *The Red Badge of Courage*. Keith was a twenty-year-old from the apple orchards of the lake country. He was a hockey star, also a perceptive, thoughtful reader.

Maybe alone in the class, Keith had recognized the vitalism on which *Red Badge* turned, the priesthood of the life force, the riddle of blood and sacrifice. Like any good, clean-living American boy, he had pretended not to know what he was looking at, and faked it sloppily.

"Henry realizes," Keith had written, "that we have within us the wherewithal to cope with each of life's challenges."

There was no excuse for it, even if down on the lake, in apple-knocker country, enough people still believed that this was the kind of lesson boys went off to college to learn.

"Read the book!" he wrote on Michneicki's paper. "Is it propaganda? Truth or illusion?"

Then he put the papers aside and turned to his computer. Encouraged by Norm Cevic, he had been spending a great deal of time trying to track his new friend Lara on the Internet.

He found her ex-husband first, a Frenchman named Laurent Corvus, a graduate of the École Normale Supérieure and the University of Geneva, assistant in Africa to the late Desmond Jenkins, a left-wing European expert on colonialism. He had begun as a secondary school teacher and then worked for the Red Cross and for the UNRRA in the Middle East. His listing was posted by a site dedicated to foreign affairs and security matters. He had occupied a few vice chancellorships and assistant directorates at some African universities. It was hard to imagine what would bring him to Fort Salines.

Lara herself, under her maiden name of Purcell, appeared on a few other sites. She was a graduate of Swiss schools and had an advanced degree from the Sorbonne. Her area of study was the Caribbean and the former colonial world in general. She had worked with her husband and also as an assistant to Desmond Jenkins.

Marie-Claire Purcell grew up in St. Trinity, a poor island on the elbow of the Windwards; her listing contained a pocket history of the place. St. Trinity was a British sugar island that supported an exotic culture of exile. In 1804, at the end of the Haitian wars of independence, hundreds of French slave owners had arrived from Cap Haitien with their property and slaves. Vodoun and various forms of the French language persisted there.

The site listed her publications: a short history of St. Trinity, a study of French colonial settlement in West Africa and the Caribbean. It went on to advertise a hotel, apparently owned by her family in All Saints Bay, in the south of the island. And it listed a number of books by her brother,

John-Paul Purcell, an authority on Caribbean religious practices. He had written and published a great deal. Lara herself sat on the board of some corporations doing business in the tropical Americas. She seemed also to connect with an entity called AbouyeCarib.com.

This site, however, was guarded by a square patch appearing in the middle of Michael's screen demanding a password. The patch was intricately designed and vaguely forbidding. He had come late and resistant to the world of the Internet, only a little less phobic about it than his wife. His one feat of electronic athleticism had consisted of decrypting the password on his son's computer, which was Falo, the dog's name backward, in defiance of dyslexia.

His plan had been to meet Cevic for lunch so they could go over whatever he had printed from the Web. There was not very much. Crossing the welter of slush and freeze between his office and the door of the deli restaurant in town, he instead decided to keep the handful of documents to himself.

Over barbecued beef, Norman complained about the college bureaucracy. He had spent the morning as the faculty representative on a committee that worked with the college employees' union. Michael listened impatiently.

"What do you think," he finally asked Cevic when they had finished their sandwiches, "about the presence of the intelligence community on campus?"

"Aha!" Norman said. It was the sort of question he relished on a topic he enjoyed. It would be hard to tell, though, how much he really knew about it.

"Are they here?"

"Oh yeah," Norman said. "They're here all right." But it would have been strange if Norman had said they weren't.

"Like," Michael asked, "where?"

"Well, you ask our new colleague about that. She works out of the late Ridenhour's shop, does she not? And Professor Doctor Ridenhour's department is surely the answer to your question. I mean," Norman said, "this is interesting. The other day I send you off to frolic with Lara. Now you're asking me about spookery. How about *you* tell *me* what prompts this question?"

"I just thought she had a very cosmopolitan background for a rustic setting like our own."

"Well, now I'm hurt," Norman Cevic said. And of course he was. Ahearn had never learned to pay enough attention. "I like to claim something of a cosmopolitan background. I've come a long way from Iron Falls. But here I am."

"You're a regional specialist," Michael said, rousing himself to flattery. "You're here for your own research. It's different with . . . Ridenhour's people."

Cevic appeared to be mollified.

"You know I worked abroad during the war," he said. "I worked all over the world at one time. The Michigan Project. Aid for International Development."

"That's why I'm asking you this question, Norman."

"Ridenhour had his great days," Norman said. "Tucked away here in the toolies but with friends at court."

Norman played with the expensive pack of cigarettes he had bought at the smoke shop in town. There it was forbidden to light one. Since he had briefly considered resuming smoking, Michael was discovering it was no longer possible to smoke anywhere. Norman held forth.

"By the late seventies the intelligence people had lost their hold on the eastern universities. Except for locations like Yale, where they were built into the bricks — but even there they had to be truly covert. So places like this flourished. You couldn't recruit in the big places — the other side made it a conscious strategy, manipulating bodies in campus demonstrations to run the Agency out. And so on. But out here the milk of patriotism never ran thin, right? The army. Military intelligence could use places like this. The uniform, the flag."

Norman kicked back in his chair, warming to the topic, the years of his provincial share in imperium.

"So, the snobs in Washington bitched that the agencies weren't getting the best people anymore. They hated to see intelligence work get to be a blue-collar occupation. They had seen the same thing happen to the officer corps. They used to say, Shit, it's getting to be like Hoover's FBI, the sons of Mormon farmers, the sons of Boston cops."

"So," Michael said, "they ended up with people like us."

"They discovered the uses of adversity. They could always operate here without much scrutiny. They could lay people off, people who were hot, keep them out here until they cooled off. For example, you'd have a guy come through, you'd discover he'd run a think tank in Hawaii, he was Bones at Yale. What's he doing here? Ask not, as they used to say. They'd send a guy here the way they used to send a promising officer to staff school, the War College. What he did wasn't necessarily what he was seen to do."

"So Ridenhour's scene was like a safe house?"

"Like a consulate. A chapter. A retreat. All those things."

"So," Michael said, "here's Ridenhour and his outfit. But the Cold War's over. Ridenhour's dead. What does life hold for these folks?"

"The captains and the kings depart," said Norman. "The peace punks are day traders online, their masters and manipulators, the young Lenins of the movement, are running departments, shoehorning their kids into Senate internships. Man, I could tell you stories. I could cite incidents. I could bring evidence to bear, man." Norman shook his head, growling.

"Nothing left?"

"Secrets, Michael."

"Secrets?"

"Maybe you can recruit in Harvard Yard again. But the walls have eyes. Places like this you can place the casualties, the burnouts, the Men Who Know Too Much. You can contain these little worlds. Beyond that," he said, straightening up, "there's damn little going on worth hiding. The Middle East action is pretty up-front in security terms. Most people are on board. What's left is the war on drugs, and nobody likes that much. It's dangerous. It's essentially boring, like it's got no cultural content. It stinks. I wouldn't look for it around here."

"I thought this was where they came when they couldn't go anywhere else."

"It's a cemetery," Norman said. Then he looked at Michael for a moment. "Except maybe for your girlfriend. She's a live one."

"You mean Lara."

Norman did a lovely bland blink.

"Did I say Lara?" He wrestled his graveled tones toward delicacy.

"You said girlfriend."

"A momentary lapse, dear boy. But I bet madame there, she's got a juicy résumé, *n'est-ce pas?* Checked it out?"

"I ran into classified stuff."

"Exactly," Norman said. "The thing would be to get around that."

Michael did not answer him.

Back at his computer, he ran Lara down to her lair behind the odd-looking logo that demanded his password. On prolonged examination, the insignia was a more ominous presentation than it had first appeared, hard to make out on the screen. It was a thing of colors. Was the red-orange shaded figure a cockscomb? Was what appeared to be a face really one? Did it have a ferocious jaw with bloodied, mandrill-like fangs? What else lurked among the dark green stalks?

The thing was unsettling. Each time he called it up, it seemed to leave an afterimage in the middle of his screen. One of those creepy things you found out there. Everyone knew the Web was teeming with them. And some aspect of this woman lurked behind this one.

Toward dusk, Michneicki, hockey-playing apple picker, showed up to discuss his paper.

"Read the text," Michael told him.

Michneicki read aloud from *The Red Badge of Courage:* "'He had been to touch the great death, and found that, after all, it was but the great death. He was a man.' So he understands that death is part of life," Michneicki declared complacently. "He matures."

"The novel is about war, Keith. It's not just a coming-of-age story. It's about the purifying effect of struggle. It's not about discovering personal identity. It's about transcending it."

Michneicki frowned, shrugged and looked at Michael for help.

"What do you get out of a game like hockey?" Michael asked him. "Does it make you feel like a small child again?"

"Huh?"

"Does it make you feel a small child? Like you're returning to infancy?"

"No way," Michneicki said.

"You're an enforcer out there. I've seen you. You like to hit people?"

The young man laughed. "Not a whole lot." He flushed and looked at his big hands. "Not really."

"Are you afraid of getting hit? Does it hurt a lot?"

"No," Keith Michneicki said.

"No. And how do you feel after a game?"

"If we win," Keith said, "great."

"Part of something bigger than yourself?"

"Well," said the young apple knocker, "the game's not about one guy."

"What's it about?"

"Winning?"

"No, I'm asking you. Is it about winning?"

"Naw," he said. "Not really. Not for me."

"How about making the beer taste better?"

"*All right,*" Keith said. "OK. Right."

"Because you've been up against it. Because you've been part of something bigger than yourself. It's a kid's game but it's not really a kid's game, is it?"

"At a certain point," Keith said, "it's not a kid's game anymore."

"What is it? What is it like?"

"Like everything else," Keith said.

"It's like life, isn't it?"

"It's life," Keith said. "But it's awesome. It's better."

"More perfect," Michael suggested. "Transcended."

"Right," said Keith.

"Take another look at the end of *The Red Badge*. Get

on the Web and search out the phrase 'moral equivalent of war.'"

Keith looked up at him from the act of writing it down. "Isn't that a cliché?" he asked.

"It's a cliché when politicians use it because they don't know what it means. Otherwise it remains a living insight. Write me something about it for extra credit. See if you can do a search for the origin of the phrase."

"My girlfriend's a kind of a hacker."

"Good," Michael said. "As long as she doesn't write the paper for you."

Michneicki packed up his notebook and his copy of Crane. Before he left, Michael said, "Ask her if she knows how to get around a password."

"Whoa," the youth said. "I don't know if she's that kind of hacker."

5

IN THE COURSE of the spring semester, Norman Cevic managed to introduce himself to Lara and ask her to lunch. They met at a dichromatically jacked-up space called Chequers with a Q, an eating house that would prove to be a local inevitability. The place catered to middle management from the handful of high-tech plants that clustered around the university. It supported a large tank full of illuminated tropical fish and for years had offered a busy, pretentious array of precooked "cuisine" that arrived at the kitchen frozen in plastic bags inside cardboard boxes, like low-grade trail mix. Subscribers to the boxed food also served the bloated lyrical menu, which was full of jokey, familiar insolence at the expense of the clientele. There were smiley managers to curse under their breath at the staff, but no cooks.

When Norman arrived Lara eased their conversation toward the subject of Michael.

"A good guy," Norman said. "Good."

"That's rare," she said.

"I wonder how rare. There's absolutely no statistical data."

"The anecdotal evidence is troubling, no?"

Norman, amused, pounded the bottom of a salt shaker. "Yes it is. But without reliable numbers we're flying blind."

"Why do you say he's good?"

"Well, let's see. He keeps his promises. He thinks about what he does. He's considerate, concerned with other people. He's a good teacher and he works hard." Norman paused to dip his fries in ketchup. "That's a start. Boy," he said, "I like the french fries here."

"Yes, they're quite well done. What else is he? Besides good."

"Married."

"So?" Ambushed, she flubbed and fluttered. "That's nothing to me, I assure you."

"I knew that," Norman said. "I assure you." He made her endure his leer. "Gee," he said, "you're actually blushing."

"To ask about a colleague . . ."

"Sure, sure," Norman said. "When I say he's married I'm not kidding. He's ruled by a strong woman. His life is circumscribed. Really," Norman said, "she's good for him. He's a lucky man." He looked thoughtful. "She truly is a great woman. Damned attractive too."

Lara shrugged to express her conditional acceptance of the possibility. He was plainly Kristin's admirer, which did not necessarily make him her friend.

"You know," Norman said, "they're giving a party next week. They're supposed to anyway — it's their turn to buy the booze. Not that Kristin wants to. But this time I think she has to play hostess."

"Going?"

He nodded without looking at her. Nearby, the Lions Club was having lunch. A little banner was in the middle of the table. It reminded her, absurdly, of the island. And it reminded her also that St. Trinity was a place as alien to her — more alien — than the forest around them now. In her St. Trin, Lions Clubs were significant. A former president had once drowned most of the membership off a principal tourist beach.

"If one of Kristin's compulsory parties is your idea of a good time," Norman said, "you can go as my date."

She thought about it for a moment. How amusing it would be. "Dear Norman," she said. "I should be delighted."

As it turned out, things were really not so bad. A woman named Arabella sang and played Schubert on the household piano, whereupon her husband recited Sonnet 128: "How oft when thou, my music, music play'st . . ." A sad, red-faced man named Mahoney drank alone. A young couple in exile from Manhattan talked to Norman about American policy in the Caribbean. Lara waited for the part about how George Bush the First had planned to sabotage the Panama Canal Treaty, but that had been dropped from the routine.

In Lara's eyes, Michael shone. He was drily funny and rather quiet, though he drank almost as much as the roseate Mahoney. His drinking surprised her. It was also being observed with disapproval by Kristin Ahearn.

She was tall and slim, with jet-black hair flecked with gray and eyes of a dramatic shade, the color of faded blue flannel. Her lips were pale, thin and unadorned. Big-boned was a suitable term for her; her bones were everywhere in evidence, like the yoke of collarbone that swelled beneath the ivory skin of her décolletage above the low-cut academic-gypsy velvet blouse. Her long lissome lower quarters were sheathed by a beige skirt in the same *volkisch* style: suede, wide-belted, tight at the hips, flaring around the knees and high enough to show her tough laced boots. A lofty, steel-eyed bitch, and she did not think much of the company, Lara included.

One thing was puzzling. Her social energy that night was concentrated on the nervous overseeing of her handsome husband. From that accusatory focus, all that seemed to distract her was the close presence of Norman Cevic. When he was near, it seemed to Lara, this tower of ivory was prey to little tremors and fidgets. A hand to the midnight-black hair, a cocking of the pelvis that shifted her contrapuntal stance. Even a little wiggle. And although it was probably Lara's imagining, it seemed to her that as Kristin leaned into Norman's space to hang upon his words, she could just possibly be angling a few soft inches of substantial, velvet braless bod where he might find them.

Did she know she was doing it? How much did she know? Lara had discovered a beautiful young boy hiding near the back stairs to spy on the party. His mother's long face and inky hair, his father's long-lashed eyes. *Un mignon,* their boy.

An elderly professor sang "The Watch on the Rhine" in German. Lara spotted Michael on his own, making drinks in the kitchen. She went over to him.

"You shouldn't drink so much," she told him. "No wonder you can't sleep."

He turned in surprise, stared for a moment and laughed at her.

"Think that's it?"

"I'm sure of it."

As she watched he put the two drinks he had been making on a tray and poured a straight shot for himself in the nearest available glass.

"In for a penny, in for a pound."

She shook her head in mock sadness as he drank it.

"I'll be your cure for insomnia," Lara said.

He looked quickly through the kitchen door, checking, she had no doubt, for the supervisory presence of Kristin. Lara turned and followed his glance. They were in the clear.

"You were spying on me," she said. "You tried to break my password. You were observed."

He looked amazed.

"Couldn't resist, Lara."

"You mustn't." This time it was she who turned to watch their backs. "Don't!" The stern look she gave him was darkened by anxiety.

The sweet singer of Schubert walked into the kitchen for ice water. Lara had a respectful smile ready.

"You have an admirer," Lara told Norman as they drove home.

"Oh yeah?"

"But sure. Kristin Ahearn."

"Get outta town."

"I am not mistaken in these matters, my friend. I'm surprised you haven't noticed it."

"But she's completely a one-man woman," Norman said.

She turned and watched him peer into the freezing night. Columns of tiny flakes whirled beyond the headlights.

"Not interested?"

After a moment he said, "I wish I could believe that."

"Norman, *cher ami*. Believe it."

He laughed to cover his confusion.

"Hey. Kristin? I don't think so."

When they arrived at her house he made no move to go in with her.

6

ONE DAY they drove as far as the Hunter's Supper Club in Lara's car, so that Michael could get his bottle of Willoughby's and Lara could see the territory. Lara drank Coors from the bottle and played Johnny Cash songs on the jukebox. It was a Saturday afternoon and the place was filling up with locals who had come to watch college basketball. They seemed to huddle at the far end of the bar from Michael and Lara, as if she had reduced them to comic peasants from a Hollywood horror movie. Their mood was restive and hostile but they behaved. For one moment Michael thought he recognized the man he had seen in the November woods among them.

"Honky-tonk," Lara observed, setting her empty beer bottle down decisively. "Charming."

Though Michael had hoped for a glimpse of her, Megan, the barmaid, was not to be seen. An obese woman with thinning hair sold him the Willoughby's. As they walked to Lara's Saab a middle-aged man with fierce sideburns and mustache appeared in the doorway. His face was swollen, pale where it was not florid. He stared at them, licking his lips urgently, at the point of giving voice to some observation. None occurred to him. Lara waved prettily.

"So this is where you come for inspiration, Michael?"

He was driving. The Saab was a treat for him.

"It's where I come for whiskey."

It was farther into the local countryside than Lara had ever been. On the way back he drove a country road, partly unpaved, that ran through Harrison County's scrubby hills and sunken meadows. The day was sunny, snowy and bright.

"My God," she said. "It's so desolate. Desolate, desolate. So far from anywhere."

"You're in Flyoverland, my dear."

"In what?"

"You've never heard the middle of the country called that? Flyoverland. That's what they call our little corner of nothing much. On the coasts." He shifted down as they approached dirt. It was a shame to muddy the car. "At least," he said, "that's what they tell me. No one ever called it that to me."

She laughed. "Flyoverland. And what would you have done if someone had called it that to you?"

"I don't know," Michael said. He thought of the fat thug they had left drooling in the doorway. He remembered the man in the woods with the useless wheelbarrow. "Nothing much." Then he added, "It's how we think of ourselves. We don't expect much."

"But all Americans have the right to happiness, isn't that right?"

"How long have you been out here?" Michael asked her.

She shrugged. "A year."

"Do you have the impression that you're among people who think they have a right to happiness?"

"But yes," she said. "They do think it. It's why they're so unhappy."

"You're mistaken. You need a good history of the settlement."

"Maybe."

"Secrets," Michael said. "Deep melancholy. Sudden death. Those are what we have the right to."

"But no longer."

"Inside, still."

"But they have God."

He glanced at her, to judge how contemptuously she spoke. It was hard to tell.

"We don't presume on God. Now we see Him, now we don't. Mostly we don't."

"No?"

"Sometimes He flies over."

This time, he could feel her glancing at him. As though he were not joking and she might have gravely misjudged him. Thrown herself away.

"Seriously. On His way to Anaheim. From Orlando."

She punched his arm. "You bastard! Teasing me."

"It's fun to tease foreigners. It's another thing we do."

"But Michael," she said, "I'm not a foreigner."

"You're a foreign-type person."

The road beneath them changed from sealed gravel to asphalt and they came out of the poor land. "Listen!"

She turned on the radio and with hardly any trouble found what she was looking for.

". . . that we have the promise of Jee-suz that he will come into our hearts and preserve us from sin! That through the day in the workplace in the street in the heart of godlessness he will be present in our hearts and we shall be armed in him and he shall be as a guide unto us . . ."

Michael leaned over and turned it off.

"That's new," he hastened to insist. "It's from outside."

She inflated her cheeks and puffed and fell silent.

Darkness came down on them still miles from town. He was avoiding the main road on the way in, trying to reach her farmhouse without passing the university and the center of town.

"Desolate," she said again. A sad winter dusk lingered over the snowy fields.

"Looks like prime soybean land to me."

"Did I tell you my brother died last year?"

"No. I'm sorry." He put his free hand on her shoulder.

"It was long expected," Lara said. "So I was ready."

"Are your parents alive?"

She shook her head.

"I'm going to have to go away, down to St. Trinity for the memorial service."

"When?"

"It should be around Easter break. It'll be a special sort of Masonic service. He was very involved in the rites. Then we'll have some property to dispose of."

"Will you be gone long?"

"Well, not really. But things will drag on for a week or so. It was an AIDS death," she added. "A pretty bad one. He had to be brave, you know. And he was."

"I'm not surprised," Michael said. "Was he alone?"

"No, thank God. His dearest friend was with him. A loyal, loving old friend."

"Well," Michael said, "thank God for that."

He did not question her further. When they got to her house he ordered Lara from her own bedroom to call Kristin; he did not want her to hear his lies. In a comic sulk, she picked up a copy of the *New York Review of Books* and went naked into the bathroom.

Sitting on the side of the bed, he listened to himself explain his absence from home, to the long silences from the other end of the line, and to Kristin's strangely soft and patient syllables.

"Sure," she said. "OK. No problem. Get here when you can."

When he replaced the phone, darkness came down on him. A loneliness he could not understand.

"It's uplifting," Lara said, emerging from the bathroom. "Sitting on the toilet seat, reading about the *élan vital*. Want to go home?"

He smiled in despair. "Not now. Hardly."

"You're stuck with me, eh? I'm stuck with you. It's sad."

"This," he said, "is where I want to be."

She stood, a hand on her bare hip, watching him.

"You could come with me," she said.

"What? Where?"

"To St. Trin. When I go for John-Paul. You're a diver, so am I. The diving's as good as Bonaire. When the rites are over we could stay at my family's hotel."

He stood silent, then said, "It's not something I do."

"No, but you could do it. There's time for you to set it up."

She walked over to him. Her eyes were a little wild. "You must," she said. "I need you and we'll have such fun. It'll get me through it."

"All right."

She encountered herself in a door-length mirror.

"And look at me. I'm shameless. What squalor. I'll put something on."

He began to protest, to insist that naked she was perfectly fine, which was true enough. She cut him off.

"Get your good whiskey because I want some. We'll play a game. I'll get you something to cheer you up."

He got up and went downstairs to get the Irish he had bought and left, for reasons of deception, untouched. He put the bottle on a tray with two glasses and a wooden bowl of ice. There was a window at the turn of the stairs and Michael paused to look outside at the first landing. The dark road, snowfields lit by a pale quarter-moon. His excitement felt nearly childlike — anticipation, surprise, guilty fear.

When he went back to the bedroom he did not see her at first. She was in a dressing room beside the closet, an innovation — like the bidet in the bath — that Lara had introduced to the rambling, Yankee elegance of the farmhouse. The holding had been a prosperous one.

"Want to hear about the *élan vital?*"

He set the tray down.

"Sure. But I don't think I want to talk about it."

"Want to talk about the soul? Are you sure you have one?"

"Not anymore."

"I think you do. I mean have a soul. I don't."

"How can that be?"

"My soul is lost. I think someone keeps it for me."

He could not see her, but it did not sound like a joke to him. It sounded, in fact, distinctly odd and a little frightening. He poured two glasses of whiskey.

"Hear her?" Lara asked. "Marinette?"

"If you like," he said. He found himself listening. "Who's she?"

"She's my godmother, the keeper of my *ti bon ange*."

"Your good angel?"

"No, love. My soul, my inner life."

She came out dressed for the game. She had made a sleek black helmet of her thick hair. She had a vest of black leather, tight trousers that might have been deerskin or goatskin, only slightly off-white. Black boots.

Where do you get it? was what he wanted to ask her. But that was not how the game was played. Laughing was permitted in some games, not all. Vulgar questions, never. He handed her the drink and she took it, doing a graceful little spin. She was never portentous about it. She had a fairly keen sense of the absurd.

As for Michael, the business did not really incline him to jokes. Her games tightened his throat, shortened his breathing, set him aching. They also consumed him with something like superstitious dread. He had come to love the fantasies she played out — if love was the word for it — but they were rooted in the darkest, most secret and ashamed quarters of his nature. They were made of the things about which he never spoke, which as often as not he put out of his mind as depraved. As crazy. Weird hits from adolescence, narratives departing from some exotic touch, something that might once have taken his attention, derived promiscuously from anything between serious art and the lowest comic strip. Somehow, she knew what got to him.

Marinette? At that moment he was thinking of the Great Whore, the perennial figure. He was thinking of Lara.

She was the great whore of their schemes, The Woman

set loose in the world. Out of control. Even in *his* schemes, in whatever it was he had once believed. But among all the fantasies and lusts, it also occurred to him, only for a second perhaps, that he wanted to love her.

"Come on, Michael. We have something good."

The something good turned out to be cocaine. The stuff was not exactly new to him; he had seen plenty in graduate school in New York. It turned up around the university from time to time, with decreasing frequency as the nineties advanced. But it certainly was not a regular feature of campus dinner parties, not even among the most earnestly bohemian. Or even of campus adulteries.

The coke was staggering and she had a lot of it, along with a couple of bedside spliffs, presumably for afterward. It made him dry-throated and jangling. The jitters somewhat dissipated his lust. He watched her walk away from him, moving quite lightly in her boots and soft-skinned pants. When she turned around she appeared to have a gun. She offered him her profile like a duelist, sighting him down the barrel.

Looking up at her from the bedside, where he had knelt to do his lines, a thrill of fear went through him. It seemed perfectly likely that she would shoot. She was stoned, crazy. Wild in the country. She would shoot them both. Stranger things happened on American campuses.

"Am I boring you?" Michael asked. "Are you going to kill me?"

"Could be," she said. "Could be, eh? Thrill killing." Delighting in the little trills and phonemes.

"Do I have time for an Act of Contrition?"

"Say it," she said. "Repeat after me. O my God, I am heartily sorry . . ."

"Fuck you," Michael said. "Kindly put the gun down."

She walked over and handed him the weapon.

"You take it."

He weighed the revolver in his hand, then opened it. There was a slug in every cylinder.

"Jesus Christ, it's loaded."

"A gun is no good if it's not loaded."

"I suppose you're a member of the NRA?"

"I'm not even Irish," she said.

He did another line.

"You know," he said, "the folks who tell you to keep your gun loaded? They also say never to point a firearm at someone unless you're going to shoot them."

"What else do they say?"

"I think," he said, "I think they say if you put a gun on the wall it should always be fired."

"How strange of them. The NRA?"

"The NRA," Michael explained, "are always confusing life and art."

"So I've violated all their rules. Will they punish me?"

"Yes," he said. "Now you've had it."

"Am I going to die?"

"I don't know," he said. "I think so. What kind of revolver is that?"

"It's a Belgian FN Special. Thirty-eight caliber. Five chambers. Firing Parabellum cartridges."

"Aha," he said. "What's special about it?"

"We'll find out," she said.

He started by taking her boots off. To take them off correctly he had to genuflect with his back to her, her leg over one shoulder while she pushed against his back with her other foot. His role reminded him of the servant in *Miss Julie*. Taking off the second boot, he felt cool metal on the back of his neck. It was the gun or it wasn't; either way, he had to admit, with all the goodwill in the world, that it did little for him in terms of erotic excitement.

He tried to remember who got shot in *Miss Julie*. She did, as he recalled. And what about the boyfriend? Him too? He was always getting *Miss Julie* mixed up with *Hedda Gabler*, Strindberg with Ibsen, a pathetic secret lapse for a man so involved with the phenomenon of the Scandinavian female. Even more compromising than his taste for armed women in skin clothing.

He allowed himself to touch the upper curve of the boot. The gleaming leather was discreetly mud-spattered, musky with the leather and the polish. Was Krafft-Ebing one person or two? Lara would know.

When he turned to her, he was relieved not to see the gun. He eased his way along the warm silky leather encasing her long legs, palms against her calves and thighs, fingering the creases of leather where the pants wrinkled behind her knees. She turned with him so he could caress the firm rotundity at the seat of those skin pants, find the cleft under the form-fitting leather.

She said something he could not understand. And how superlative it was to feel her tight turns so exotically sheathed and hear the sound of her voice and have the taste of her mouth, her whole body pressed against him. The entire sense of her concentrated where his hands explored. When she was out of the trousers, in her black bikini pants, already wet, he went down on her, obliging with his tongue the precision she required. And then she on him, and he felt quite in control but avid indeed.

When they came together after that, she had the gun again.

"Shit," said Michael.

"I want it," she said. "I have to have it. You're the only one I can do this with. You love it, I know you do."

"No!"

"Yes, yes," she said, and she guided the gun against her belly and his hand to the trigger housing and all he could think of was the safety, but he had no idea whether the circle around it showed red.

"What if I get what I deserve?" she said. "What if I get the slug there?"

That would be a story all right, long and difficult in the telling. But something — he thought it must be her trembling intensity — made him want it too. Crazy. She touched his prick.

"I'll lose it," he said.

He felt her turn the gun on him. He closed his eyes, terrified.

"You wouldn't die alone," she said.

He reached down and took the gun away from her very gently and put it on the floor. The safety was on. They did what they had done the first time, exploring, probing, penetration. No secrets, no shame. Nothing he had ever done came near it.

"Crazy," he said. He was trembling and laughing. Maybe crying too. "What are we doing?"

She began to recite: *"Und wir? Gluhen in Eines zusammen / In ein neues Geschöpf, das er tödlich belebt."*

She reached out and touched his jaw and turned his face toward her. "Yes?"

"Yes. I mean, sure. Yes. What does it mean?"

"You'll look it up. It's Rilke."

"You'll have to write it down."

"Remember," she said when they were in the shower. "You mustn't use my soap. She'll smell it on you. Use the little hotel soap."

Then it was time for him to go. He dared not look at his watch. She walked him to his car. It had started to snow and the lights of her house caught the first intermittent flakes. So beautiful, he thought, looking at the delicate snow. So peaceful. So suggestive of the world he had once known, before the snow had become his enemy. The world that had been lovely, presided over, though it passed understanding.

"We have to have a meeting on Phyllis," Lara said.

"What?"

"The committee. Phyllis Strom's thesis committee. We have to contact Fischer."

"Yes, of course."

"We should set up a lunch. E-mail him, get him in the loop."

"Right," Michael said. "We have to do that."

"Oh," she said. "You wanted the quotation as well. Why don't I get it?"

He looked at her blankly.

"The Rilke," she said. "You know!"

"Oh," he said. "The Rilke. For sure."

"So," she said briskly, "let me just jot it down. For you. But you have to get the translation for yourself."

"All right," he said. Yes indeed, these little *jeux d'esprit* of the scholarly life are so wholesomely refreshing. And, bustling, she ran inside and got a Post-it pad and wrote down the verse and stuck it to his sleeve like a badge.

"*Voilà!*" she said. She touched his arm as he removed the sticky note. "Good blow, eh?"

"Oh," he said, "the coke," and saying it aloud he looked around him in their isolated place, guiltily wuss-like in his own aware observation. "Socko!"

"So we'll save the spliffs for next time."

"Right," he said.

"Soon, my love."

"Yes," he said. "Soon."

He drove home at about thirty-five miles an hour, the way he had driven stoned in college, creeping around the campus, speed bump to signal to stop sign.

Once home, he parked outside his darkened house. No lights had been left on for him. The darkness froze his heart. Not even a bulb over the door.

He tried to close his car door without making too much noise. Slamming it but not slamming it, doing it but hoping he wasn't doing it, the story of his sorry life. The front door was locked, so he had to use his key. He stood huddled against the dark shape of his own house, searching blindly through his possessions, before a door it seemed he had let shut on him forever.

7

THE NEXT WEEK, Michael came into the kitchen to find Kristin at the table, straightening out a yellow Post-it note that had been rolled into a cylinder. Her glasses were on her forehead. She put them on to read it.

"*Und wir?*" she read. "*Gluhen in Eines zusammen / In ein neues Geschöpf, das er tödlich belebt.*"

She looked up at Michael, then back at the note. Trying to translate it aloud.

"And we . . . glow as one . . . made new deathly . . . renewed." She looked up at him again.

"And we," he declaimed helpfully, "we glow as one. A new creature, invigorated by death."

"Whose writing is this?" she asked.

"It must be Phyllis. She sort of . . . made a note."

Kristin looked at the note again. "We glow as one?" she repeated. "Invigorated by death? Phyllis?"

Michael shrugged.

Kristin stared at him. "The little twit must be losing her tiny mind."

"It's Rilke," Michael said.

She soundlessly determined the meter. "OK. So why did she give it to you?"

"Just a note she made. I guess I ended up with it in my pocket."

"It was in your pocket all right. I sent those pants to the cleaners."

"Good."

"I mean, it sounds like some kind of suicide pact, doesn't it? Is she all right?" But it was Michael she was attentively examining.

"Oh, I think so. We're discussing vitalism."

"Oh really."

She was on her way to some kind of upscale Bible study class a few of the women had formed. It involved studying Greek and reading patristic literature. She had bought Calvin's *Institutes of the Christian Religion* from some Web site in Canada. She had another book, about the Synod of Dort.

"Literary vitalism."

She sighed, but he could not tell whether the sigh represented exasperation with the wrongheadedness of literary vitalism or over something lost. It moved and wounded him, reminded him that he loved her.

"By the way," she said when he was at the door, "should you perhaps have a conversation with Paul?"

He had no idea what she was talking about, but the suggestion of required explanations made him uneasy.

"About what?"

She pursed her lips and looked at her watch.

"You've been absenting yourself."

"I've been busy."

She nodded impatiently. "Sure. Well, this is sort of sweet but it's causing him terrible angst. He's being ragged about a valentine he sent a girl in his class."

"Oh God."

"The little bastards at school have it," she said. "They're driving him nuts with it. One of the kids managed to get it off the teacher and circulate it and they won't leave him alone."

"Poor kid."

"Listen, Michael?" She sounded faintly desperate. "Why don't you see what you can do in the way of paternal guidance."

"I'll look for a chance," he told her.

"You know," Kristin said, "he's much more innocent than other kids his age about this stuff."

"Yes," Michael said, "I realize that." He put his mouth under the kitchen tap to drink.

"You know, my dive club is sponsoring an excursion to Grand Turk this Easter break. It's a great dive. The Puerto Rico Trench."

He did not turn to look at her.

"Well," she asked, "could you take Paul? He might like to snorkel."

"Unfortunately not. It's adults."

"Oh really? All boys?"

"No, no. Not at all. You could come if we could get your mom over."

"Mom's pretty frail. I don't know. No, I won't go." When he looked at her she seemed so without suspicion that it quickened his guilt. "I guess you go ahead and do that one. It is a shame," she said, "that you can't take him."

"It is. I'll make some time for Paul and myself this spring."

He drove to his office and stood at the window. The night before had brought him terrible dreams. In squash games with Lara and Kristin, two furies, he struggled for breath. Most fearsome of all was a Lara-Kristin figure, a goddess enraged. Loaded guns were used in the form of squash they played; the court was fouled with dirty snow. A painted man with a wheelbarrow watched. Everything in the dreams was somehow true. There was a voice to tell him that, or if not a voice, an informing narration that commented on the dreams.

In real-life waking squash he was beating Lara as often as not. There were games that he put every fiber of his strength into winning.

"Stalingrad," he had said once, taking a long hard point from her.

Michael's office window commanded a view of the main college plaza. The day outside was insipid, gray and chilly with the foreclosing of a brief thaw that had brought buds to the beech trees along the walks. Students, dressed down to hurry spring, kept their eyes on the path, all of them headed somewhere they would rather not be. The ugly brick block of the campus bell tower showed a length of painted sheeting advertising a party. As he looked at the tower its carillon bells began to play "Abide with Me."

He had always enjoyed his office. There was a fireplace, rectory lace curtains, a high stamped-tin ceiling. There were family pictures on the mantelpiece and a northern pike displayed on a wooden plaque — something had possessed him to mount it. How idiotic it was. Rural idiocy, said Marx. Or someone.

Late, she rang him.

"Meet at Chequers at four, yes?"

She was half an hour late; she was always late, he had discovered. The bar was filling by the time she arrived, but in spite of that, in spite of the dimness and the gloom of afternoon outside, her presence ignited a slight charge in the room. He knew the effect. As a young man, his own physical attractiveness had cast its modest spell, though awareness of that had come to him late.

She had on the dashing fur and tailored faded jeans that resembled no other pants in the state. She stood in the doorway for a moment and then came to the banquette where he sat boozing. He helped her off with the coat. She ran her lips against his cheek.

The day's confusions cleared in that instant. He was very glad to be with her. He went to the bar, picked up a plastic basket of chicken wings and sauce and brought them to the banquette.

"Want some?" he asked her.

She daintily lifted a wing on a plastic fork and made an insulting face at it. "How can you?" she asked. "Merciful God."

"They're not *that* bad." He polished one off and wiped his fingers. Cheering up.

She shrugged. "One day I'll explain to you about food."

"Pointless. I lack the necessary standards." He looked into her tolerant disdain and laughed at her. "You're so arrogant," he told her. "You're absurd."

"Am I? You think so?"

She put her hand on his thigh, in his lap, and stroked him, looking cool as midnight. "We'll have to play squash again, eh?"

"We must."

He called for another drink, ordered her a martini.

"We're off for this weekend," she told him matter-of-factly. "I have to go to Washington."

"Why Washington?" he asked.

"Oh," she said. "Business with my brother's estate."

"Too bad," Michael said. "Me with my ready excuses and all."

"Remember what they were, Michael. You're not a good liar. No doubt we'll need them again."

Back home, he let himself in as quietly as possible. He stood listening for a while without turning on the light. The house was quiet; he concluded they had gone to bed. Guided by the embers in the fireplace he eased himself into a living room chair. As he did, his foot kicked over what turned out to be a half-finished glass of beer. It was unlike her to leave half-consumed comestibles around. There was an open book straddling an arm of the chair. He looked at the title in the dying glow: *An Introduction to Kierkegaard*. Kristin approached everything with native caution. The book was open to page vii, so she seemed to have stalled on the introduction to the *Introduction*. But she would get there.

An intermittent sound outside caught his attention. Drawn by it, he put on his jacket and went out to the garage. Standing by the garage door, he heard the noise again. A muffled thud, a resounding of metal followed by something like a scattering of rain. Cars went by. The sound came again, followed this time by the screech of brakes and a skid. A car door opened and slammed.

"Motherfucker!" a male voice shouted. "I'll kick your fuckin' ass."

He heard the crunch of running footsteps in the snow and another chainsaw burst of profanity. Then the car dug out in a series of squeals and the driver gunned the engine. Michael zippered up his jacket and went in the direction of the footsteps.

The night outside was cloudy and there was no moon. A line of evergreens separated the quarter-acre of yard beside the house from the road it fronted. He walked to the closest tree and saw a figure motionless against the pale phosphorescence of a soiled snowbank. Immediately he recognized the figure of his son.

The sight of Paul in the snow triggered unreasoning panic. Yet instead of calling him, Michael watched and waited. Paul was crouching behind the bank, chipping away at the side of it, gathering up the icy snow and packing it into snowballs.

When the next pair of high beams lit the road, Paul raised himself for a quick look over the jagged parapet. As the car approached, he pressed himself against the snow wall, cradling a supply of snowballs like an infantryman with a string of grenades. At the crucial moment, he stood up and let go with the chunks, passing them left hand to right, hurling them sidearm at the passing car. After each throw, he shouted something Michael could not make out.

Michael took a few measured steps over the snow toward the boy's position. Another car came up; he hung back. Watching Paul, he could tell even in the darkness that the boy was in distress. After releasing the last snowball of his fusillade, he would crouch and clench his fists and utter the little cry. Then the last car went by untouched and Paul was out of ammunition.

"Paul?"

His son stiffened as though struck. He spun around and took a false step as if to run, first to one side then to the other.

"Hey, buddy. Just be cool."

Paul doubled up, weeping. Michael walked out and put an arm around his shoulder and started walking him inside.

"Don't you think you could cause an accident doing that?" He spoke gently and his easiness was unaffected; he was not angry. "Do you want someone to run off the road?"

Paul pulled away from him.

"Ice can break a window, man," he said. Paul broke for the house and vanished into it.

Michael followed him in, waited a few minutes and then went upstairs to Paul's room. The room was dark and Paul was huddled under the quilt. All of his bedtime rituals had gone unobserved. No time for a read from the books neatly tucked beside the lamp, no notes to himself in his mother's scrupulous hand. His teeth went unbrushed and there were no evening prayers. Michael was not about to push it.

"I hope you know," he said, "that you can talk about anything with me. The troubles you have are very likely to be similar to the ones I had. Often it helps to talk." He did not really expect a reply and he did not get one. "And of course your mother is here for you too."

All the same, he could not keep from trying again.

"Sometimes you think, Why me? But we all make the same mistakes usually. Everybody feels awkward sometimes."

At Paul's age, he thought, he would have been told: Offer it up. Redeem the world through your humiliations. He had always thought that brutal, but all at once it did not seem so bad. It was a way of making children believe their suffering could mean something.

In the darkness before his son's room he felt the vertigo of the shifting world. Stop, he thought. Go back. To the sweet order that had prevailed when life was innocent and carefree. Standing there, he could almost believe things had been that way. Of course there was still time.

8

S HE FLEW first class from Minneapolis on their money.
They allowed her a small suite at the Mayflower and,
for the last time, she thought, a uniformed chauffeur
waited behind the security gate at Reagan National. She
thought it might be a good idea to register the chauffeur's
face. The day might come when she would be desperately
avoiding him at airports, hiding. He was a huge-shoul-
dered *cholo* with a Chac mask of a face.

As he put her single bag in the trunk, the thin lines of a
smile displaced his stone god's countenance. He had permitted himself a small joke, a wee merry observation to
amuse the pretty passenger. But Lara's Spanish, normally
quite workable, failed her under the traffic noise, the takeoffs and landings in process all around them. Whatever
he had said got by her. When he saw to his horror that his
sally had fluttered and sunk, he swallowed his little smile,
stuffed the remnants and odd angles of it back into the
dusty earth of which his face was composed. His fierce
black eyes flashed fear.

For the rest of the ride Lara tried, in various ways, to reassure him. The people he worked for disliked jokes in
general, and unsuccessful jokes roused them to fury. They
liked jokes to be theirs, at the expense of others; otherwise
they sniffed disrespect and treachery, which they believed
always accompanied the telling. Dealing with them, Lara
was beginning to discover that humor, if it was not their
sort, could represent humanity and mercy to the forces they
served. It was preserving holy water against their infernal
ambitions. Irony scattered them like rats, though never far
enough.

The car drove her straight to the house in the Virginia
hills. She wondered whether she would ever see the suite at
the Mayflower; the prospect of spending the night enter-
taining her host in the big house was loathsome.

The place was a Greek Revival plantation home. It had
spotless columns and pastures with similarly immaculate
fences stretching to the foggy hills. There was a horse or
two. She wondered if they might be Argentines. The green
grass was icy and the reeds in the marshes stiff with frost.
There were patches of unmelted snow at the north end of
the pastures.

Lara was praying that the chauffeur had not been in-
structed to take her suitcase out of the trunk. He made no
move to do so. A tall butler with an English face opened the
door to her. She told him good afternoon.

His answer was in native Spanish. A cold greeting, something *para servirle*. They went into a long carpeted room
with chandeliers and sofas. The tragic faces of Creole gen-
erals from the wars of liberation hung from the pale yellow
walls. Someone had encouraged the old senator to sit for a
portrait, which presented him like El Greco's inquisitor,

with crumpled papers at his feet, shod in alligator boots. Undoubtedly sugar-quota bills to draw contributions for his election campaigns.

A woman appeared, a motherly sort, wearing a black apron and a belt full of keys.

"Only this bag?" she said of Lara's handbag. Lara handed it over. "Would you like to freshen up?"

The woman followed her up a flight of stairs to what Lara was displeased to see was a bedroom. It had a fine view of the grazing horses and the blue ridge.

"The bath is to your left, dear."

"I'll need my handbag."

"*No hay problema*," said the woman with a smile. She snapped it shut and handed it over. Had she searched the bag for wires, weapons? In any case, she returned it.

"I thought I was staying at the Mayflower."

"*Claro que sí.* Tough to get accommodations there, but we did it."

They smiled at each other. There was no further searching.

"*Para servirle,*" the woman said.

Lara spent as little time as she could in front of mirrors. She did what she could to dull the scents of Northwest Airlines and made herself relax. The search, she reminded herself, was for cameras and recorders, not for weapons. It had not come to that.

All at once she found the mirror held her. She looked into her own dark, almost green eyes. On the island, in the parts where she was remembered, it was believed that Lara had no soul.

Many believed it. People said her dead brother kept her soul with him under the waters of All Saints Bay. In Guinee.

They said that he had offered it to Marinette, the wild woman whose murderous rage had made her a *petro* goddess centuries ago. They said that Marinette occupied and enslaved her.

It was also speculated that her husband, a living man, the Red Frenchman, kept it; that Fidel himself, a *santero* and servant of Elegua, kept it in an emerald. Or that Marinette, in some spectral reversal, had taken it to Africa, where it labored digging for emeralds, to atone for Lara's family's mistreatment of their slaves, and that was why Lara always appeared tired and could not always remember the things that had happened or what she had done.

At the worst of times, when it seemed impossible, when she dreamed of La Marinette night after night, when she wanted to die, Lara went to the mirror and begged and laughed and cried for her soul. Sometimes she sang, French songs, African songs, Jim Morrison. Sometimes, like the servant she had seen that day, she had to swallow her songs. Once, in front of the mirror, she had tried to hang herself. Hard work, day and night, in the mirror without a soul.

There were times she could swear she did not appear there, when the person was unknown and the room some dreadful room adorned with coral fans and armor, altars to the Virgin and Child, or to other figures perhaps — Mamaye, Agwé, Elegua, Ogoun. Maroon saints, mutated Taino predators, their lizard tongues pressed against the mirror for a taste of the pale fishbelly white, her soul in Guinee.

There was one thing, one hope. No one had ever said her soul was forever lost to her, not forever. And there were times, plenty of times, when she did not believe such things at all. As a little girl it had been all right. The first few times, when she saw La Marinette or Guinee in her mirror in the years before, she had laughed. She had made it a game to terrorize the girls in her Swiss school, to make them see her as exotic, bad and dangerous. When she went back to the island, Sister Margaret Oliver, who had her own beliefs about the mysteries, told Lara not to worry.

On her way downstairs Lara saw portraits on the walls that had not been there during her last visit, the sort that looked painted from photographs. George Orwell. Arthur Koestler. A few patriarchal figures she did not recognize but who she guessed were Latin American military men. One might have been Pinochet.

Downstairs, something like a board meeting had been taking place. About a dozen men in Italian suits were drifting out of the conference room. There were Anglos, Hispanics, a few Afro-Latins. All were men, and a few she recognized. There was a young Haitian American who worked on the staff of a senator. Also a good-looking Cuban American lobbyist who, it was said, had written every line of nearly every bill introduced by certain members of Congress for the last ten years. His prose reflected the interests of his clients, who were frequently offshore corporations. The men stood in groups around the reception room while the butler ordered up their cars.

The Cuban approached her. Frightened as she was, it was good to see him. She always had a weakness for Cuban charm.

"Hi, Lara. Traveling south?"

She shrugged and kissed him.

"In a good cause, I hope."

"*Semana santa,*" she told him, for some reason.

"Shall I introduce you before everyone's gone?"

"No," she said. "It's hopeless."

He wished her *buena suerte*. She wished him the same. He held her eyes for a moment. She greeted the Haitian American Senate staffer, a young man of the elite. The two men turned away to speak with each other and another man she knew joined them, an American who represented some evangelical foundation.

"So," the Cuban American told his colleagues, "I said to them, Listen, you don't want that guy on the Foreign Relations Committee. Why? Hey, the guy's an Arabist. We want him out of there. *Ándale,* fucker."

"But Pablo," the smooth Haitian American said, "he's not an Arabist at all. It simply isn't true."

"I beg your pardon," the lobbyist said. "He wears little pointed shoes. I sat next to him on the subway. They curl up at the ends. He's a Muslim terrorist. His opponent is a God-fearing yokel, *un hombre muy formal.* This is the war on terror."

The American, a God-fearing yokel by profession, laughed agreeably. Lara, smiling, took a chair to wait for Triptelemos and tried to listen to other conversations. Men spoke in English, Spanish, French.

She saw some members of a scholarly organization that had flourished in the Reagan era. They were a remnant now, but once they'd had money and power to spare, and Lara, following her ex-husband's lead, had gone to work for them, attached herself after leaving the great Desmond Jenkins and the service of Soviet disinformation. By then, no one cared who had killed Hammarskjöld, that Mobutu dined on human flesh. South Africa was giving way, the truncheon falling from the Boer's ham hand. There was a slaughter of the Eritreans; Cuban soldiers brought AIDS home with their Orders of the Red Banner. Islam appeared, rampant.

She and her husband ended up assigned to a catchall outfit, run by fanatics, increasingly short on money and power, increasingly lawless. It had been a mistake; they had been badly handled by the French, who had no use for them and passed them to the Americans, by which time the Cold War in Africa had shrunk to a few plague spots of starvation and murder, marginal in the world's eye. But it was all she had been able to promote from the free world end of the great blighted battlefield of Phantom World War Three.

For his friends, the Haitian American read archly from the translated newsletter of a right-wing racial nationalist on a colonial island who reportedly had been receiving funds from every major intelligence agency in the world.

"It's called 'Le Message du Soleil,'" the young man explained, and read on:

"'The African sun alone was the quickener of the civilized instinct. From Africa, it spread to the Fertile Crescent. But, *hélas,* not before it attracted the attention of cold pale dwarfs, a stunted race, mean of size and frigid of heart. Cunning and cruel. I refer to those known to the world as Caucasoids, otherwise as *blancs.* The white race, *enfin.*'

"Present company excepted," the young Haitian paused to say.

"Wait a minute," one of the Americans said. "This is *our* guy?"

"Big tent, Arthur. Many mansions." The young man looked at them for leave to read on.

"'Yet the sun alone,'" he continued, "'was font and symbol of vitality. Thus, in an outburst of energy, one leader of the whites, perhaps the most gifted, took as his sign a dim stick figure of the sun. For what was the cross, my friends, if not the sun? And in his hands twisted it to its true likeness, to invoke the bright bounty of the great star itself.'

"He means the swastika," the dapper young man added helpfully.

"Yes, I caught that," the Cuban said.

The Haitian kid cleared his throat.

"'Rousing his crippled race to demoniac energy in its name. This leader so wickedly great, one — all — must admire him. Even as one recognizes him as the foe to emulate. So one day, as the trumpet notes sounded for Siegfried, the drums shall proclaim a leader for the sons and daughters of the great sun, the children of Amon Ra. Though I shall not be here to see it, in my soul's vision I see it now!'"

"My word!" said the American.

"That's just the way he sees it, Arthur. He's a good man."

"*Adiós* and farewell!"

Lara recognized the voice she had been dreading. He was an Argentine former military officer named Marcial Pérez, who liked to call himself Triptelemos.

"May our affairs prosper." He went to stand at the door and sent them off with *abrazos*. Not everyone who braced for an *abrazo* received one.

Once there had been a great secret coming and going, people leaving by separate doors without formality. But now the men from Triptelemos's meeting ambled casually past the butler to wait for their drivers. Perhaps the organization had stopped trying to conceal its influence and was trying to magnify it. Heretofore money had been collected in secret, but that might change, Lara thought.

When no one but Lara and Triptelemos remained, he approached, half bowed and kissed her hand.

"Did you see them admire you on their way out?" he asked her. "They thought, Who is this mysterious beauty?"

Lara laughed. "I could have told them, one of many. Just another mysterious beauty on the big *estancia*."

Triptelemos ordered tea and they adjourned to a small parlor to have it; English tea, Belgian waffle cookies.

"I always imagined 'waffle' was an American word," he told her. He repeated it, waddling his jowls. "Waffle. Invented in Pittsburgh when a foreman spills his lunch on the factory's iron floor."

When she did not respond he said, "So sorry about your brother. Everyone expected you to go down for the funeral."

"I couldn't," she said. "I mourn him, believe me. But the place I teach, it would have been difficult getting someone to fill in. And I'm new. I mean, it was impossible, believe it or not."

"I believe it," Pérez Triptelemos said. Triptelemos was a name he had acquired on acid many years before, although he looked not at all the type. He claimed he'd been given the LSD by Arthur Koestler, who had known Timothy Leary. She thought he might have got it in Buenos Aires from a CIA collaborator with the dirty war. His play name had something to do with spreading grain, fighting communism. An acid vision. He believed in some variety of neofascist revolution, and Lara had found herself one of his mysterious beauties.

"We expected after your brother's death that there would be something for us."

"You know, I guess, we're selling the hotel? Roger is

dealing with my brother's collection of island art. I'll be going down to help with that."

"We wondered," the officer said. "What about the rest? We have to pay the Colombians."

Lara understood that the hotel organization had connected itself with one of the right-wing Colombian militias. Her brother had worked with them. They had used the hotel and the island in their operations, although Lara made it her business to know as little as possible about it.

"Roger's running things now," she told Colonel Trip.

"Roger? Oh yes, Roger." He seemed to laugh good-naturedly. "Roger." As though he were taking satisfaction in his benign tolerance for all mankind.

"John-Paul trusted him."

"Therefore we do the same. There's a ceremony of commemoration, is there not? Perhaps I'll attend."

She stood amazed, afraid she must have gone pale. That *he* would be on the island! The thought petrified her.

He patted her hand. "Only in spirit. I wouldn't dream of intruding on those rituals."

"You've been kind to us," Lara said.

"Our work . . . this part of it is coming to an end. But there will be other strategies and other battles. *Compañeros* fight on in Colombia. With your brother gone, we vouchsafe our trust to you and the Colombian brotherhoods."

"You know, Triptelemos, I've left the work. We're selling."

"Yes, I know." He went in his pocket and took out a jewelry box. When he opened it, she saw the emerald and took it out.

"Señor!" She looked at him, and with the look mustered

all the supine female deference of which her mind and body were capable. Her soul was in reserve.

"It's African," she said. "It has the oil." She ogled it until her eyes watered. "Oh, señor!" She leaned forward and they kissed with both cheeks.

"Now you have to tell me," he said to her. "You must be truthful. Did Fidel give one to you?"

She only smiled.

He lowered his eyes. "I'm indiscreet."

He began to talk about the situation on St. Trinity. Even without her assistance he seemed well informed.

"You know the American presence down there is extensive. The intelligence services of the old regime can't even tell us where they are. Wherever Junot's army is in the field, the *yanquis* are with him. They seem to control the roads. So you and Roger will have to get on with Junot. The Americans ask him everything."

She wanted to tell him it meant nothing to her. Of course she knew better. Ironic, she thought, that a charmless torturer like Trip should appeal to one's confiding impulses.

"So," he said, "Junot will speak to the Americans, the ones who matter. Roger Hyde will speak to the Colombian militias."

"Roger is almost ready to retire. When the hotel is sold he'll return to Mexico." That was the way she wanted things to go.

"Perhaps he can cooperate for a while. A few stones to the malls of Boca and Hilton Head. Until the debt is paid."

Lara nodded. When the interview was over, the man who called himself Triptelemos clicked his heels, in the style of his national army.

"Good luck with your American protectors," Colonel Trip said. His saying it alarmed her. It made her wonder how much he truly knew.

Triptelemos, they said, had read French poetry to the people he was taking out to drop, alive, into the South Atlantic. His crew would push them out at the moment the disk of the sun disappeared over the horizon. Or else the moment the disk appeared. He had a handkerchief to dry their tears. Sometimes it was a wife's handkerchief, the scent suddenly recognized by the condemned, a cruel recall in the dazzle of the horizon. Or that of a husband, or a mother.

"I confound the wise professors," Triptelemos liked to say. "I make the machos cry.

"Sometimes," he would say, "they are so like children. Children again, and I am their father. 'Papi?' Sniveling, no sarcasm now. 'Are there sharks?' We would reassure them. 'In the South Atlantic? Off this continent? Never. You will see.'"

It was after ten when she arrived at her suite at the Mayflower. In time for the last subway, she went out. Nobody seemed to be observing, but it was finally impossible to tell. Walking toward Dupont Circle, she found a public telephone and called the dummy number.

On Connecticut Avenue she took the subway to the Zoo, then walked back toward Kalorama. There was an Ethiopian restaurant on Newark Street, still open, still serving a mixed clientele of East Africans and Washington After Dark. In a rear booth, a young woman in jogging clothes was drinking nonalcoholic beer. She had long, straight black hair, quite dark skin and Semitic features. The woman really might be anything, Lara thought, taking a seat across the table from her.

"So what's this?" the woman asked her.

"This is life after John-Paul."

"Yeah, we know that," the young woman said. "Tough. AIDS, right?"

"So," Lara said, "this is, We never did what you thought we did."

"Fuck you didn't."

"We never did what you thought we did. People on the Hill could have told you that."

"Uh-huh? Oh really?"

"And we are out of it now. Out of it because we're selling the place. I mean, check it out."

"You know what? You're not out of it. We'll tell you when you're out of it. My man got your ass skinny-dipping with Fidel on his wall. Picture's right under Mr. President's. You owe us something."

"I take a risk, you see. To set the record straight."

"We keep the records. We'll set *you* straight."

"You're so rude," Lara said.

"Yeah," said the young woman. "We're just policemen. We don't have the background."

9

ON A SPRINGLIKE Sunday full of sparkling sunlight and warm confiding breezes, the Ahearn family went to Mass. A little before ten o'clock, the three of them trooped up the slate steps of St. Emmerich's. It was a white wooden church whose central structure stood flanked by twin pointed towers tipped with Prussian blue. St. Emmerich's was a German foundation, different in every subtle way from the Frenchified Irish church across town.

They went single file, Kristin tall in the lead. One step behind, Michael trudged eyes down, containing his sick hangover. Young Paul followed him, looking abstracted and melancholy, occasionally rousing himself to a few moves of the insolent swagger he was trying to practice unobserved. He had brought it home from school.

At the top of the steps, Michael turned to look at him.

"What's the matter with you? You have a sore back or something?"

Paul straightened up but declined to answer. Watching

closely, Michael thought he saw a second's glint of un-
focused defiance.

He followed his wife into the sensory explosion of
stale incense, varnish, old wood and lilies. The church inte-
rior was a pattern of grays, no sculpted altar but a stark table, the simple mensa, on which two candles burned. Each
opaque gray window held a single decorated pane showing
a stylized icon. Behind the sacrificial table a sanctuary lamp
glowed before a gray banner displaying the Chi-Rho.

Michael stepped aside to let his wife and son into the
rear pew he had chosen. Paul genuflected and crossed himself. Michael and Kristin blundered into eye contact, exchanged a bleak unseeing glance and sat down.

From his place Michael could watch the church fill.
There was always a small colorful contingent from the university. The aged Professor Doroshenko, a philologist and
an immensely learned authority on Slavic myth, led his
failing wife to a place near the front. The professor's many
tomes on wood sprites and river elves were regularly released by an émigré press in Winnipeg. Behind the
Doroshenkos Mr. Giorgio and Mr. Cushing, a pair of middle-aged gay librarians of signal piety, knelt in prayer. Beside them sat Dr. Almeida with his wife and four of his children. The prolific doctor was a Goan and a savant at the
computer center. Then there were the few dozen students,
whom the church did its best to make welcome. They were
mostly young women, away from home for the first time.

The rest of the congregation consisted of the townies and
farmers. Three, sometimes four generations, descendants
of the nineteenth-century Rhenish and Bohemian settlers,
still showed up each week, ancients and babes in arms.
The rural churches were being closed and consolidated; cir-

cuit-riding priests equipped with folding communion sets and cassettes of *Tennessee Ernie's Sacred Songs* spent long weekends holding Mass in half a dozen ruinous sanctuaries among the rows of soybeans. Only a scant fraction of the family farms remained out there.

The Germans were lumpy-faced and broad-shouldered, clear-eyed and scrubbed. Their young folk were freckled and fair, possessed, it seemed, of a radiant innocence.

Across the church, he saw a man named Harold Lawlor, who with his wife, Frances, constituted the dynamic of the local anti-abortion struggle. Michael put his glasses on and assumed an easy stance from which he thought he might observe Mr. Lawlor at his Sabbath devotions, telling his beads, eyes raised in the Maiden's Prayer.

Lawlor's elderly cousin, a man named Brennan, had shot a priest in South Dakota — crippled him for life — for permitting a twelve-year-old girl to assist at Mass. Brennan had insisted on altar boys; it was said he had spent the day of the shooting stalking the twelve-year-old, whose young life was preserved from his nine-millimeter bullet by chance. The plea had been Alzheimer's. Brennan was eighty and had died the same year. A martyr.

Watching Mr. Lawlor's watery blue eyes fixed on the numinous, Michael gave way to a spasm of rage; his jaw trembled. His fists contracted to claws. He had to remind himself that this man was not the shooter. As Michael watched, he completed the last decade of his rosary. Oh, the sorrowful mysteries! thought Michael. Lawlor crossed himself with the chaplet's crucifix, kissed it and fixed his rheumy gaze once more on unending bliss.

The celebrant priest, short, square Father Schlesinger, read scripture.

"I will go to the altar of God," he declared. And the pale, buzz-cut server, kneeling with the soles of his Reeboks toward the congregation, replied, "To God who giveth joy to my youth."

Beside Michael, Paul was praying. Decently, head down, following the order in his missal. The storms of impending adolescence had for the moment subsided. From the look of him, Michael thought, he was making contact. Casting the line up there, bending the reverent eye on vacancy, discoursing with the idle air. He saw the boy clasp his hands to his chest the way he had as a small child, and indeed, as far as Michael could tell, took hold of something and hugged it to his heart. Acknowledged and confessed it, rejoiced and partook. Outside, spring birds that should not have been present at that latitude warbled and trilled.

On his left sat Kristin; Michael saw that she too was watching Paul as he prayed. They could not take their eyes away. Their son was alive, the guest, like everyone, of random singularity. Random singularity, a mere machine, required no sacrifice. Yet around them secrets ascended with the incense and song. The farmers and clerks and cops, the professors, the young women on their own, all of them fought to merge their desperate inner lives with the peace that, it was written, passed understanding.

Finally Michael stood at the point of trembling, burning with shame and self-despising rage. The church that taught humiliation as a blessing was providing him all the humiliation he could bear. He regretted ever having led his son into its fragrant candlelighted rooms. He thought of Kristin in the hospital, leaning on the God she had conceived, imploring the mercy of dreams. He wanted to be out of there. Once, his mind wandered from a fit of anger and he imagined that there was a tiny old lady beside him, a doll-like creature with a death's-head smile. Marinette. She smelled of sachet. One of those waking dreams in the empty space he had come to church to contemplate.

Driving back, the best he could do by way of Sunday meditation was the picture of Lara among coral arches, her long body gliding past luminous tendrils or against the silky surface.

They went home to the ancient hum of after church. Pancakes for the young communicant. Ice water and the Knicks-Heat game for himself. Kristin took off her church clothes and put on a pair of tight jeans that caught his attention. He stood at the front window ignoring the basketball game, watching her rake winterkills in the yard. Those warm curves at the hip and the choice ones at the seat. The center seam taut, deep in. It was strange, ever since Lara had come into his life he had been in a state of sexual tension that focused itself equally on the two women. He was in different ways besotted with both of them. The high-pitched ache of desire was always one sensation away.

When she came in he thought she must know the way he had been watching her. All she said was, "What was the date of that dive charter?"

"Twenty-fourth. Easter."

"I guess it'll be nice there."

"Want to come?" He wondered if he had not hesitated too long on the false question.

"Shall I?"

"Sure," he said, "if you want."

"Yeah?"

So he wondered: What are we playing here?

"I just know," she told him, "you'll have a better time without me."

It was not quite what he had wanted to hear.

10

IN SAN JUAN, Lara played number 18 with five-dollar chips, covering it from every possible angle: corners, lines, neighboring digits, plus red, middle twelve and even. After four spins of the wheel it connected. She followed that by betting thirty-six covered and won.

The jolly croupier congratulated them. Michael saw her wink and slide him a fifty-dollar chip.

"Come on," she said. "I'm buying."

The service to St. Trinity had been suspended before they landed in Puerto Rico. There were difficulties subsequent to the election there, and the army had divided against itself. The airline treated them to a night at an Isla Verde hotel. From their room sixteen floors above the beach, they could hear the breakers but Lara was eager to hit the tables.

Nice-looking Puerto Rican teenagers in evening dress rushed breathlessly through the corridors, outrunning their families, who were talking over each other in a doubling of languages. After Lara's win, they found a bar that overlooked the rocks at the edge of the beach. It had tables set in a grotto surrounded by bird of paradise plants and traveler's palms. The place seemed agreeably cheerful, as though all intrigues were for fun and jungles were places for sipping cool drinks under the tropical moon. There was one of those as well, almost full, silvering the reef. The lights of San Juan made it look like a city without a care.

She raised a glass. "The founder of the feast, his memory."

Michael drank carefully.

"You're not to think I'm callous, Michael. Or that I didn't love my brother. I've told you I mourned him."

"I wasn't sure you meant John-Paul. I thought it might be some gnome in Washington."

She only looked at him, not answering. He took a lighted candle from another table so that they might have more light.

She was on the phone in English, French, Creole, getting tickets out of San Juan; she did it all with the fortunate smile that won at roulette. "Let's go back to our room," she said, "where I can really get on the phone."

When she was on the bed, between desperate phone calls, he lay down beside her. "Is there something more you should tell me about our trip?"

"Like what?" she asked him. After a while she said, "Where to begin?"

"Maybe begin where the papers leave off," he suggested. He had been following the story, though she never spoke of it. His strategy had been not to mention anything out of St. Trinity until she did. The stories in the *Miami Herald* that morning described burning roadblocks and lawlessness. He put his glass down and stared at the ocean.

"Don't look so worried, Michael. Everything will be with us. I do love you, you know. That's why I asked you to come."

"I came because I wanted to be with you, Lara. I could go back tonight if I wanted to." In fact he wanted to share a taste of danger with her. To descend as far, to take as much of her as he could survive, and risk even more.

"Are you mine in the ranks of death?" she asked, laughing.

She wrapped her leg around and under his. He moved close and put his hand against her, against the wet silk and strands of hair.

"You see," she said, "it isn't a question of life and death. I don't believe that. I'm not really asking for protection. Just the company of someone I've come to care for."

Her tone seemed to have changed ever so slightly since he had first questioned her.

"Whatever you need," he said, "whatever I can give you . . ."

"I've told you we're selling the hotel, right?"

"I assume the hotel was funded in some way," Michael said. "To political purpose."

"Yes, and now I'm trying to collect my very small share. After the service, after our goodbyes sort of, we're dividing who gets what. I can take care of all that. I just didn't want to be on the island completely alone."

"You said you had an American passport?"

"Yes, I have American nationality through my mother. My father's family owned the hotel since it was a sugar mill. Since there were slaves. Like a lot of people on the island, my father's family came originally from Haiti in the nineteenth century. They brought slaves with them."

"But they were white?"

She smiled and shrugged.

"On St. Trinity, Purcell is an important name. But on the highest levels of colonial society" — she shook her head in mock sadness — "not tiptop. And a lot of the old colonials would tell you: Purcells? Wonderful people. South part of the island. From Haiti, you see. Touched here and there. French. Creole, see?"

Michael nodded.

"All I can tell you," she said, "is my granny was never asked to leave a Pullman car in the southern United States." He looked at her solemnly. "Damn, Michael," she said, "John-Paul used to get a laugh with that."

She told him that she expected no trouble but that she would be carrying valuables home, and the political situation there was extremely volatile. Everyone who read the papers knew that.

"Also, my brother and his partner were in business with some people in South America and I don't know how hard they want to contest the final count. I'm not expecting violence or anything. I don't want to be unaccompanied."

He thought back to the tropical gargoyle guarding her on the Internet.

"We'll be arriving separately," she told him. "So there are a few things you have to remember."

That they were arriving separately was news to Michael.

"Why separately?"

"Oh, it fell out that way. They had a seat on the American flight to Rodney, so I put you on it. I think I may have a seat to All Saints Bay by way of Vieques." She took his hand. "Don't look so abandoned, poor baby. We'll fly back together. The thing is, I have to get there for my brother's rites."

"Funeral rites."

"No, the Catholic ceremonies are over. These are local. Masonic, sort of."

"Presumably I'll see something of you on the island."

She closed her eyes and did the anticipation of bliss.

"From Rodney you have a bus ride," she told him. "People are very poor. You're beyond their sympathy. Watch your bag every minute."

"I could rent a car."

"I wouldn't. Alone."

"Even in daytime?"

"A rogue will get you at the first pothole. A laid-off soldier with an expensive weapon. Take the bus or even an omni. It's not Haiti, but these days it provides a few bad moments. But we know that, eh?"

"Yes, we know that. I hope it's a pretty ride. Rainforest."

"A pretty ride," she repeated. "Yes."

"Of course I understand that the road might pass through a lot of local trouble this week . . ."

He realized that she was cutting him off.

"Let me tell you something, Michael. The Masonic rituals are island things. Local practices. They're not like anything you've ever experienced."

She lowered her voice and looked into his eyes.

"Let me tell you what people believe. They believe that the souls of people who died the year before are taken to a place under the sea called Guinee. After a year or so the souls are brought back from the sea. That's what our ceremony is for."

"All right," Michael said. The traditional nature of it all comforted him.

"My brother was a volatile, restless man. People believed he had special powers and that he could do wicked things."

"Did he? Do wicked things?"

"People believe that he gave my soul away. That he gave it away to an old woman called La Marinette."

"Your godmother."

"She lived centuries ago," Lara said. "I belong she. I belong to her." He was looking into her eyes as she spoke. "La Marinette," she repeated in a whisper. "She began the killing. She drew the first French blood."

"And you want your soul back."

"I have to ask John-Paul to give it back when we take his *ti bon ange,* his soul, from Guinee."

"Lara," he said slowly, "I think you have a perfectly good soul, quite intact."

"No," she said, "you're mistaken. You've never seen me. In a way."

"That can't be," Michael said. "Then everything between us would be illusion." When he said it, neither of them moved. He considered what he had said. At the base of it was a simple thought he did not dare to complete.

She held his eyes and covered his mouth with her fingers. "I am free to love. To love more. I love you beyond death, I swear."

"Beyond death isn't necessary."

"Maybe it is," she said.

"I got to believe you," Michael said, mocking them.

"That's something people say."

"Yes. I say it. Here I am."

"Truly?"

"Yes, truly."

"Look," she said, "that's all I can explain. Tell me you won't leave me now."

"You know," Michael said, "we were supposed to go diving down here. That was the original intent."

"Oh, yes," she said. "We will go diving the best. We'll dive the most beautiful reefs time has ever seen."

He thought it a strange way of putting it. But then, perhaps to illustrate time, he put her hand against his body, had it descend the wall of his belly.

Just then in the hotel room, the soft lights of the Old City visible in the window behind her, she seemed frail and anxious as he had never seen her. He felt a distant stirring of madness somewhere. Not Lara's necessarily. Nor his own. Not anyone's madness, maybe just a different arrangement of things over some horizon.

"All right," he said. "As long as we get to go diving."

"Oh yes."

Their telephone rang and after a moment's hesitation Lara answered it. She spoke to a woman in excited Spanish. With the woman still on the line she put her hand on Michael's knee.

"Michael, I can get a flight by way of Vieques if I leave this minute. It's one seat but I have to be there for the reclamation. You know why. I mustn't miss anything. Will you forgive me if I take it? Please?"

"Of course," he said. "Go ahead."

Back on the phone, she cheerfully disposed of Michael's future and hung up.

"And you're confirmed on the flight tomorrow to Rodney. Don't miss it."

"I haven't missed a plane or a bus or a train since I was eleven."

"Well, don't miss your bus in Rodney." She brushed his hair to one side. "It's going to be a shock after the Caribe Hilton. Don't forget to watch your bag."

"My bag would be a disappointment to marauders."

"Don't joke, my dear, because it *is* dangerous. Stay by the bus — there'll be a security guard there. Everything in Rodney is rent-a-cops. Don't try to be a sophisticated traveler, you'll be killed. When you get off — get off at the market in Chastenet. Go to a shop run by a man called the Factor. He's not a real official, but he can tell you where to find the Bay of Saints Hotel. Most people are sweet. When you get to the hotel, stay there."

"All right," he said. "I guess I've got it."

"No," she said, "you haven't understood what I've told you. I can see that you haven't."

"Do you mean about the bus? You were clear enough."

"I don't mean about the bus. I mean the other things. You don't understand a word I'm telling you."

"It's not my world, Lara."

"And it would be easy for you to go home. To leave me here and go back to . . . everything. But you must come with me."

He tried to consider everything. Everything seemed lost, traded for something rich and bright, a deeper darkness, alien light, dangerously insubstantial.

"Yes, I'll come." He felt as though he were lying; at the same time he knew he would follow her. "Of course I will."

11

FROM THE VERANDA, Lara could see across the high walls studded with spikes of many-colored glass that enclosed her family's house. The view was one she remembered from childhood: the sky, the blue shades of the bay, the mountains beyond. That morning she was up at daybreak. The early-morning fragrances lingered until the sun had cleared the Morne and lit the green peaks and the brazen geometry of the mountains.

The night before, after the flight, she had been listening to drums from the ruinous Masonic lodge in the nearby hills. They had sounded through most of the night.

It seemed to her that when she was small there had been more birds and that they had more agreeable calls. Now there were hordes of crows, along with the vultures she remembered, clustering in the high palms. On the landward side of the house, smoke from charcoal fires almost obscured the overhanging peak. The top of the mountain was a ridge of bare rock.

"I listened to the drums last night," she told Roger Hyde.

"Did you dream?" Roger asked her.

"Not at all," she said. "It's all like a dream here. It seems so strange."

"It's not a dream, baby. It's a mistake. You shouldn't have come. Especially on one of those flights."

Roger Hyde had gone to Harvard with John-Paul. He had been her brother's companion since their twenties and had spent nearly all of John-Paul's last year on the island, bringing medicine, persuading the American doctors from the medical mission to treat him.

"I've come to get what belongs to me. I have a right."

"I never thought of you as greedy, my dear."

"Don't be ridiculous," Lara said. "I have my needs here too."

Roger went and stood where he could see the rutted road that led down to the smoky plain and the sea. He stood watching.

"You're beautiful, Roger," she said. "If I were greedy I would take you. I would take you by force."

Roger's father had been a historical novelist, an African American from Boston whose books romanticized the antebellum South and were perennial bestsellers. Their heroes were spurred, booted cavaliers whose gallantry and imagined swordsmanship quickened the pulses of garden club ladies throughout the southern states. Hyde *père*'s novels had been often filmed by Hollywood, but the author's picture never appeared on the book jackets.

"And I would surrender," Roger said. He looked worried, but hale enough. His life suited him, she thought.

Roger's mother was French and the family had lived in Mexico. For a while Roger had tried writing in his father's genre, continuing the formula. After the first few novels it had not worked out. The themes had become embarrassing. So he had come from Mexico City to live with John-Paul at the Bay of Saints Hotel, to write travel pieces and interviews and to help with the daily administration of the place.

"Look, you should take what you think is yours and go. I'm very serious. It's quite dangerous here."

"I thought I'd do a little diving. Also, I brought a friend down."

"Are you joking?" Roger asked her. "You must assure me now. Tell me you're joking."

She had no assurances for him. She explained that Michael Ahearn would be flying in shortly.

"You know that Eustace Junot's army is defending the election. He has the Americans. Besides that, it's total disorder. Looting and daylight robbery."

"It sounds like the ocean is the place to be. I'm going swimming."

"Lara!"

"Roger," she said, "this is me. Your friend Lara. John-Paul's twin in the mysteries. I have to be here for the *retirer.*"

"I thought you had forgotten all that, sweetheart. Why don't you?"

She shrugged and smiled. "Not possible."

"All right," he said after a moment. "I'm seeing the European Union observer late this afternoon. There are things we need to know. Want to come?"

"After my swim."

"And you'll get to meet our associates, because they're coming in."

"Are they like the pilot I flew in with? He was silent the entire time."

"They're like that," Hyde told her. "Reserved."

She changed and went down the ancient stone stairs to the water. The shore was rocky and littered, but she had caught the pure morning light, still unmuddied by smoke and the sun. As a little girl, she had been told to throw a stone in the water to honor the god. If she forgot, the girl minding her always threw one in.

She tossed a clean stone and said the god's name. Agwe.

Working her way past bristling colonies of sea urchins, she flipped and somersaulted over the edge. She knew the reefs and rips from childhood.

The water felt good, calming and elating at once. She felt strong and composed, although she missed Michael. The prospect of the rites, though she feared them, excited her.

Dazzled by the sun, she had headed too far from shore. She treaded water and had a look around. She could feel velvety staghorn beneath her feet — the middle reef. Her brother's secret beach was around the nearest cove; with a businesslike crawl she swam past it. Halfway, she turned over and shifted to a backstroke, pulling herself along handful by handful, navigating by the slow clouds drifting in on the late breeze. Half a mile away, beyond the coral tips and visible only on the outgoing tide, was the wall that descended toward the source of creation, the place the Maroons called Guinee, purgatorial Africa, where death was better than servitude and untended souls awaited visitation, salvation, home. In that place the angry dead danced with Marinette.

Fishermen and loafers on the shore, mothers and wading children, watched her. Though she had not been to the island for more than a year, she had the feeling they knew who she was and where she was headed. She pushed on. Memory came on the taste of the ocean, the force of the withdrawing tide. Now and then she rested on her back. A diver, she was comfortable on her back, pushing along with a rowing stroke.

When she was a girl the island was a paradise without a snake, if one was a certain kind of person. Her Royal Highness appeared on the money, and the American State Department took a cheerful view of local graft.

And she, Lara, was a little white princess (practically, almost entirely), and the island, as the nostalgic saying held, was as safe as your bathtub for such as she. But history prevailed even in Paradise, a term for the island that passed gradually out of use among the most fatuous of flacks, and the ongoing curse began to sound its drums, though the cry in the street was only half heard. At first, *la violencia* was a new Colombian thing. Nobody owned a Walther — a cutlass sufficed.

One night at a diplomatic reception in Rodney, a handsome Frenchman approached her. He was a teacher who worked on the island with an educational foundation. In his white dinner jacket, Lara thought he was the most dashing figure she had ever seen, serious but charming. Everything about him seemed dramatic, yet not in the least theatrical.

"You're not American?" he asked her when they had been introduced.

"No." She denied it. Why not? How disagreeable to be one.

"A Creole, like myself?"

On French and Spanish islands, local white people sometimes called themselves Creoles. On British islands, never.

"Yes," she said. Curiosity led.

He turned toward a visiting American, a pleasant middle-aged baldy.

"See that man, Lara? This happy fellow?"

Smiling, she turned, expecting to be impressed.

"With these, their hatred of the darker races is the closest thing they possess to a sense of honor."

She stood for a moment still smiling, blushing, until she was able to speak.

"What a horrible thing to say!"

"Beautiful Lara," the Frenchman said. "Come and see our work in Williamstown. Our school. And I will go on saying horrible things until you believe them."

Something about him impelled her to forgive his frightening bitterness. She wanted not to come within the compass of his rage, to be forgiven. He claimed to be a Cuban; he had changed his nationality to be one with progressive humanity. She was considering her claims. You could be anything you wanted in Paradise.

"This term I teach every day at St. Brendan's."

"We'll find a day," the handsome Frenchman said.

She had married him and they had gone to Paris. Then she had become, as was said, an agent of influence, a tiny auxiliary of the socialist bloc, under the tutelage of her husband and the great Desmond Jenkins, the wizard of influence agentry in the Third World and at the United Nations. She had met Castro and Graham Greene. She had known their company.

Then she and her husband had changed sides and been bartered by the French services to the Triptelemos brigade. Bad luck, and now, she thought, it would be remedied, the hotel sold.

What was most important was that at John-Paul's *retirer* she might reclaim her soul, which he, her brother, had teasingly given over to the keeping of his own protective spirits. He had done it to punish her for going away to school in Switzerland, and for other things. She was in love, it seemed; she thought of Michael's body with pleasure. But the best thing was that she would be whole again.

Silvery barracuda darted around her in the inshore water. A pod of brown rays rose from under the sand as she waded out of the mild surf.

By the time she had showered and changed again, Roger was gone. The house had a floating population of servants and hangers-on, none of whom were anywhere in sight. The telephone was working and she called the hotel. Michael's flight from San Juan had not taken off. No one knew about the bus service to the capital.

The keys she had brought with her from the States still served their purpose. Checking the garage, she found the old Land Rover with three quarters of a tank of gas, not enough to make it to Rodney and back. There were some jerry cans of gas but she was afraid to drive the roads with them. If Michael needed fetching, she decided, she would go. Then, on impulse, she set off along the coast road toward the convent where she had taught school. On the road she passed no one except an elderly woman who was closing her soft-drinks stand, padlocking a battered tin shutter. A few miles farther along, a gang of young boys shouted after her.

As she pulled up at the gate, she heard the sounds of a football match inside. When the old Haitian servant let her in, she saw the game itself in progress on the parched field: two sets of teenagers playing Gaelic football. One side had been equipped with rugby shirts. Their opponents, playing bare-chested, showed the knotty frames of the poorer island people. Lara parked her machine in front of the two-story school building and watched for a while. On a veranda on the upper story, she saw Sister Margaret Oliver, in dark glasses, apparently absorbed in the game, poised on the edge of her rocking chair. It was so very like her, Lara thought, to set the boys at Gaelic football behind convent walls in the middle of an insurrection.

Another weight of memory stopped Lara on the way upstairs. The hallways still bore the foreign schoolroom fragrances she recalled from years before. Metal polish and candle wax, ink and cut flowers, ant spray and English soap. When she stepped out on the balcony, the nun was shouting something in Irish to the boys on the pitch. Lara paused before knocking on the frame of the louvered door.

The sister shouted down to her *spalpeens.* Her side, Lara thought, must naturally be the shirtless ones. Lara felt herself in a welter of all the crazed, promiscuous forces of her island. Nuns shouting in Gaelic to black children playing Irish games. Cane cutters singing in medieval French patois to the rhythm of their cutlass strokes. Here and there plastic radios running on tractor batteries playing rhythm and blues. From the school balcony, canefields stretched toward the purple ridge of the Morne Chastenet, where the descendants of Haitian Maroons served vodoun *loas,* African gods and savage Taino spirits in thin Christian disguise.

Meanwhile at St. Brendan's, for a hundred years the Marist nuns and brothers had been urging black and brown children to prodigies of valor at Gaelic football, shouting encouragement in the *auld* speech. Of course they had to offer cricket as well — the island passion — along with the sermons of Cardinal Newman and the speeches of Edmund Burke. During the seventies they had somehow obtained *Manchild in the Promised Land* for the library and a New York gang novel called *The Cool World*, these beside Winston Churchill's *History of the English Speaking Peoples* and devotional pap like *The Glories of Mary*.

To go with religiosity and mildly Whiggish history there were manuals of etiquette and forms of address, so that should a St. Brendan's student wish to correspond with a marquess or any person of like degree, the appropriate salutations could be referred to and applied. Lara had ordered her third-form class to read *Uncle Tom's Cabin* together. It was still popular.

But during Lara's time as a teacher, the Marists, with the bishop behind them, had struggled to suppress the dread Rastas and their dread hairdos and the trappings of black power, which Sister Margaret Oliver called American rubbish. Eldridge Cleaver and Frantz Fanon had turned up on the library shelves in that period, the Fanon courtesy of Lara herself.

Noticing Lara's presence in the doorway, Sister Margaret turned and removed her round-framed dark sunglasses, so grotesquely fashionable on an old nun, more than slightly sinister, suggestive of American rubbish.

"Oh, dear Lara! Oh, bless you, darling girl."

Lara tried to keep her from standing. On the field there was an outcry; someone had scored.

"Goal," Lara said under her breath.

Sister Margaret shook her head in wonder. She called down to the referee.

"Jack? Can you carry on without my support, do you think?"

The young black man who was refereeing gave her a thumbs-up sign. The nun ordered tea from the country girl who served in the kitchen. There were no hugs and kisses. Irish Marists and their students refrained from embracing.

"Do you really think it's safe to have them all in today?" Lara asked. "I mean, shouldn't they be home?"

"Not at all," the nun said. "Not at all. The junta would be putting rifles in their hands. I'm keeping them here until Junot and the Americans get it under control. Not that I'm cheering, you'll notice."

"You're not for the junta, surely?"

Sister Margaret laughed. "What? With us responsible for Colonel Junot's education? He was one of ours, you know. An alumnus."

"Of course."

"But I don't want my lads used for target practice, and these walls have faced down as many armies as there are in the Book of Kings." She had a look at Lara. "I suppose you've come back to close the hotel."

"Yes, I'm saying goodbye to it all, sister. I won't be coming back."

"Well, you know I'm surely sorry to hear that now," said Sister Margaret. "I thought when I heard you were coming home to us . . . I thought what stories she'll have to tell. And there'd be something to do in the evening besides watch American rubbish on telly."

Tea arrived in its good time, hauled rather than carried upstairs by a petulant and out-of-breath teenager, over-weight and surly.

"I hoped you'd come and teach here again," the sister said. "Now that you'd seen the world."

"How nice that would be," she said. "No, I've taken a job in the States. Political science."

They both watched the panting servant girl withdraw.

"You should have gone to medical school," the nun said. "You might well have done."

Lara smiled. "You had my life planned."

"I passed the time planning your life, Lara." She seemed really to be weeping. "Don't worry, it was a good life I planned you." Outside, the boys shouted again. Lara was touched, only for a moment, with grief and regret. It seemed she must be picking up the old woman's mood swings. Grief, regret and fear too. "Well now," said old Sister Margaret, sniffling aside her disappointments in Lara, "political science, is it? And in the States."

"I wasn't doing anyone any good in Africa."

"But you were! You were needed."

"I was a Soviet agent, sister."

Sister Margaret Oliver looked around to see if they had been overheard.

"Is that a joke?"

In fact, Lara couldn't help laughing. "It's true. Desmond Jenkins recruited us. My husband as well."

"You shouldn't say such things, dear. This government is run by the CIA." Margaret Oliver had a second look around. "Ever since the Yankee intervention. You could get thrown in jail."

"I'm sure they know all about me, sister. And you too," she said, meanly teasing. Outside, there was another cry of "Goal!"

"What?" demanded Sister Margaret. "What, me?"

"I'm joking, sister. They're really not that efficient. People who studied in Cuba are back in the government now."

"Dr. Desmond Jenkins," Sister Margaret said, "was honored everywhere. All over the Third World. Even in America. I can't believe he was a spy."

"He wasn't a spy, sister. He was an agent of influence. He helped the Russians to look good in the English-speaking world. He was paid for it. And for exposing the Americans."

"Exactly," the nun said. "Exposing them, so they called him a Communist, as they always do."

"Well," Lara said, "Jenkins did better out of it than poor Laurent and I. We were supposed to be agents of influence as well. But we lived on our university salaries. Old Desmond had his tax-free honoraria and lecture fees."

She told Sister Margaret a bit about her divorce.

"We were fond of each other," Lara explained. "But half the time Laurent was assigned to the Francophone countries there, and I had the English-speaking ones."

"He's older than you," Margaret Oliver said equitably.

"Yes," Lara said, "there was that."

"How is it," the nun asked after a moment, "how is it, considering, that the Yanks will give you a visa? And a teaching position."

It was a sly question that involved some compromises and complications. Lara gave her the simplest answer.

"Mum was American. So am I, sort of. I was born in New Orleans, so I have an American passport. Kept it up-to-date but never traveled on it in Africa. You can use a UN diplomatic passport there if you know how it's done. Desmond taught us."

In fact they had both defected from Desmond Jenkins's Bolshevik fan club. Her husband had gone to the French secret service, Lara to an American foundation. Jenkins had died teaching in America, a high-living gay deceiver of most uncertain allegiance, passed away with the Cold War. Practically, Lara thought, the week the Wall went down.

"So," she asked her old teacher, "is history God's will?"

"God's plan is what we are measured against," said the nun. "History is what we perpetrate, God help us."

They sat listening to the play outside.

"Do you believe in *les mystères?*"

"That is theirs," Sister Margaret said unhappily. She nodded toward the field where the boys were playing. "It's not for us when we have . . . all that we have. Our religion and our knowledge."

"Only theirs?"

"They are old — very old things," Sister Margaret said after a moment. "They are left over from Creation. From darkness, almost."

"Almost? Are they wickedness?"

"Not wickedness," the nun said. "In the darkness, for them to find their way. Everything leads to light."

Automatic fire echoed off the range of the Anse Chastenet.

"The thing is," Lara said, "I'm involved. It was John-Paul. He always felt like a twin to me. He confined my *petit bon ange.* You know, he had the powers of a *houngan.* He pledged my soul to Marinette."

Marinette was a figure of rage and violence. Not a god but a woman who had lived once. A terrible godlike raging woman. She belonged to *petro,* which her brother had favored, the violent side.

"Did it change you?" Sister Margaret asked.

"I feel her. I feel without a soul sometimes."

"God will help you if you ask. God is stronger than these spirits. They're like the *sidh,* as we have at home."

"Anyway," Lara said, "I go to the *retirer* the next few nights. And I hope that . . . it will come back. You know how hard it is to talk about this. You can't explain it to people. I've tried."

"You're so strong," Sister Margaret said. "So clever. Keep your eyes on heaven. Their power will fall away." She took Lara's hand and whispered something, a phrase that might have been Gaelic or Creole. "The Woman's Blessing on you. She crushes the serpent underfoot."

"I shall be happy," Lara said. "I feel it."

12

THAT AFTERNOON Lara and Roger drove over to the Bay of Saints to visit the lounge and try to get a measure of the situation. The only guest in the hotel was an elderly Dutchman named Van Dreele who had observed the elections for the European Union and was following through with a report on their general effects. Van Dreele always stayed at the Bay. It was far from the capital at Rodney and mainly lacked the working faxes and armies of rent-a-cops available down there. But the food was good and Van Dreele had his own reliable sources of information. Every second day he would be driven the length of the highway in one of the blue and white UN cars to have a look at the capital and the lay of the land between. It was easier to sort things out at the Bay.

When Roger and Lara arrived at the hotel patio they found Van Dreele busily lining up his apéritifs. He had been in Rodney the day before, and all morning e-mails had been arriving threatening his life.

"Threats here used to come with a headless rooster in a

burlap bag," he told Lara. He was taking lunch in flip-flops and an outsized yellow bathing suit. "Now one gets an e-mail."

"Which is worse?" Lara asked him.

"Harder to delete a chicken," Van Dreele said, stroking his tragicomic mustache. "Of course things were more prosperous then. No one has roosters to spare these days."

"Is Social Justice going to take over?"

"Junot and the Americans. This time they'll make the vote stick. But the junta will do what they always do."

"And you'll stay through it all?" Lara asked. She restrained a lick of his wild white beachcomber's hair. Sun-bleached locks fell over his wide forehead.

"Anyhow, I'm too old to be afraid. This is what I tell myself."

"Don't take them personally," Lara said.

"They're against my person," the Dutchman said.

The threats promised what was piously called in Haiti, whence the style had originated, "Père Lebrun," and involved being burned alive. It was hard to be dismissive of them at any age, and Van Dreele was a brave man. Some said he had made it his business to atone for the Dutch at Srebrenica.

Madame Robert, a local woman who had progressed from assistant chambermaid to housekeeper, came over to tell them that the press would be visiting. A young American reporter named Liz McKie, a Miami feature writer and specialist on the area, had made a reservation and hoped to join them.

"McKie?" Lara asked. "Isn't she the one we don't like? Did you know she was coming?"

Roger nodded.

"Miss McKie and the Bay are not friends," he said. "However, she's the companion of Eustace Junot."

She tried without success to call Junot from memory, but he had left St. Brendan's before her time, a scholarship winner, packed off to prep school in the States.

"Eustace is the man charged with Americanizing the Defense Forces. So turning his good friend away is not the thing. Anyway," Roger said, "you may find her fun."

"I find her attractive," Van Dreele said. "I tried to hire her as an assistant, but unfortunately Eustace found her. He's going to be our local André Chénier. Toussaint. Bolívar. She will commit it all to history."

"I suppose we don't have to comp her?" Lara asked. "She's not a travel writer."

Roger shook his head. "On the contrary. We set them up for Miss McKie."

Lara thought about it. "You know," she said, "Francis has a way of undercooking goat that's really disgusting. Maybe we should gut one in her honor."

"Francis's goat is lovely," Roger declared, "and I'm going to miss it. No, Miss McKie is a fucking ascetic. She gets too hungry for dinner at eight. She stays in the lowest hippie hovel in Rodney. Freddy's Elite."

"All the hip white kids used to stay there."

Roger nodded bitterly. "I should know, sweetheart."

"No kidding, Rog. You picked up white boys at Freddy's? That's a switch. Who paid?"

"Sometimes," Roger said with a sigh, "the trade was distinctly rough."

"At least," Lara said, "she didn't invite us there."

Van Dreele stood. They could hear a car pulling up in the hotel's turnaround.

"I don't want to talk to the press," the Dutchman said. "And McKie is a minefield. By the way," he told them as he went out, "Junot's secured Rodney and the whole south part of the island. His troops will be up here in a few hours and they have some American support units. Also Special Forces with the forward elements."

"That means," Roger said, "we'll have a lot of hungry ex-soldiers up this end of the island. This is where they'll hide out." He waved cheerfully to Miss McKie, who was coming up the stairs. "We've got to get over to the lodge and get this over with. Things are coming unraveled on this island republic."

Lara gripped the table. "We have to get there by night-fall," she told Roger. "For *retirer.*"

"I've hardly forgotten," Roger said. "We'll deal with McKie and go."

She meant the ceremony for John-Paul.

Miss McKie had worn khakis and sandals to join them, along with a navy blue T-shirt and a knit sweater against the night breeze. She was pretty; her slim neck and delicate features made her look like a dancer, but she was not tall. The candlelight at the table suited her. She appeared very much at home, which was not what Lara had expected.

"I'll never recover from the beauty of this place," McKie said. "I won't forget it."

"And now," Roger said, "you have attachments here. The Caribbean moon makes all irresistible." He was referring to Eustace Junot.

"I understand your father was Roger Hyde, the novelist," McKie said quickly. "That true?"

Roger smiled as though he were listening to something far away, hearing different words.

"All that old-time swashbuckling stuff, right?" McKie persisted. "The gallant South. But you didn't live here or in the States?"

"We lived in Cayoacán," Roger said. "Down the street from Trotsky."

McKie gave him a long-toothed smile. Then she turned to Lara, looking her over somewhat impolitely.

"I understand you teach political science at Fort Salines, Miss Purcell."

"Call me Lara."

"Do you deal with the modern history of this island? The corruption and poverty?"

"I'm afraid we can't stay long, Liz," Lara said. She brushed her shoulders and tossed her head as if she were cleansing herself of Liz McKie's effrontery. "We haven't time for the grand historical questions."

"My questions," McKie said, "are all about modern history. Independence to the present. May I ask a few?"

"We're afraid," Lara said, "your close connection in the Social Justice Party — and the Defense Forces — would shade your interpretation. And we have an engagement tonight."

"Actually," Roger interrupted, "if I were you, I would get back to my friends."

"We inherited a historical situation here," Lara said. "We all did. Everyone. We're in business here, we have been for two hundred years. We pay a decent wage for a day's work. Higher than any of the offshore American or European companies."

"Is it true that you're involved in moving drugs to the United States?" Liz McKie showed the same smile.

"There's never been a drug case connected with St. Trinity," Roger told her. "Not one. All local businesspeople are accused of it. Whereas American-owned companies are said to be pure. Why is that?"

"Informed people say it. They say there's a political dimension."

"Do you want to stay here for the night?" Lara offered. "The roads will be troublesome if you're traveling after dark."

They got her in her car and under way. Her driver was one of Junot's American-trained soldiers, and he looked worried as he drove out of the hotel's turnaround. Miss McKie sat in front, beside him.

"A stupid waste of time," Roger said when they too were back on the road. "We've got to get the shipment out whether the Colombians have arrived or not. The pilot's been standing by."

"Waiting for darkness," Lara said. "Same fellow I came in with?"

"Truly," Roger said, "I try not to distinguish one from the other."

"I won't ask you about drugs," Lara said.

"You needn't. People don't understand how it is."

"No?"

"You know," he said when they had left the road and were struggling along rainforest track, "we also have a reputation for *not* moving drugs. At least we used to. We're in the arts business primarily. People ask us about emeralds."

When the quick darkness fell, the drums began.

"I'm hopeful, you know," Lara said. "I have a blessing and I'm determined that nothing go wrong."

Manhandling the wheel, Roger glanced over at her and smiled.

"What?" she asked.

The drums were louder and closer. They heard the ogan, the metal roarer, lay down a commanding beat and the other drums fell into line around its tempo.

"You're so like him."

"Ah," she said happily. "Twins in the mysteries."

"I hope nothing goes wrong," Roger said. "I hope you see him."

13

T HE PILOT was a Colombian-born Basque named
Soto. Until learning to fly a few years before, he
had been partners with his brother in a wholesale
electronics business. The business had thrived but he had
found the life boring.

As darkness came down on the mountains, he stood by
the wooden benches outside the lodge, smoking, listening
to the drums. He knew Lara slightly from the short dead-
head flight down from Vieques. He had delivered a new
plane from the dealer, a lovely Beechcraft that pleased
him, evoking Bogey and Ilsa at the Casablanca airport. The
plane that he would fly north was fueling on the edge of
the canefields surrounded by armed men. Colombians and
other off-islanders had replaced the local security, in which
the higher-ups were losing confidence. It was a good plane,
a Cessna 185 taildragger of the sort useful for rough-and-
ready takeoffs and landings, worked on that morning by an
expatriate Cuban mechanic who had a little cigarette and
rum factory outside town.

"Sit if you like," Lara told the pilot. She was preparing herself for the ceremony that was under way in the *hounfor* and she had been trying to stay out of his way. The sound of the drums had brought him over. He looked from the drummers toward the ruinous lodge building.

"It's strange, this."

She shrugged. He took out a pack of cigarettes and offered the opened pack to her. She declined.

It was strange there even to those who had seen a great deal. The lodge was a nineteenth-century building of stucco and brick, with a tall steeple and three Ionic columns in front. Above the formal entryway were painted the *vevers* of the gods around the Masonic square and compass. It stood in what was now an abandoned village of Haitian-style thatched houses. The canefields around it had been cut back to provide a grassy landing strip, at the far end of which was a low tin-roofed machine shop, painted in camouflage colors.

"It's how it is here," she told him.

The *hounfor,* the temple where they would reclaim John-Paul Purcell, was pitched against one wall of the lodge building. It was constructed of leaves and branches. At its center, running from the earth floor to the thatched roof, was a wind-twisted snakelike pole called the *poto mitan,* representing the serpent of wisdom, Dambala, whose sinuous form connected earth and heaven.

The pilot gave her a knowing grin. She had no idea what the look conveyed. Some kind of grim complicity, taking no comfort and expecting none in return.

"*Buena suerte,*" she said, smiling.

He was flying north this time. Roger had decided to send everything out before the island dissolved in chaos, with the Americans and their friends closing down airspace.

From the *hounfor*, Lara recognized the words of the rosary in Creole, sung against the iron meter of the ogan, a plow beaten into sounding shape. The opening of the prayers to the Virgin were chanted by the *mambo,* a market woman by day, priestess of the night now. As the crowd chanted the response, the beat of the *seconde* took up its place in the prayer.

From across the field, she watched the pilot toss his final cigarette and cross himself. She had seen the boarding gesture many times before in that part of the world, and she rather adored it — the operatic heroism of certain of the pilots, lean solitaries in the inimitable Spanish mode. Though they always seemed to toss the cigarette at the nearest fuel line, their blessing enclosed a small moment of humility before they mounted and went forth. The Yankee pilots did it differently: their heroic model was Chuck Yeager, their style was conventional — another day, another dollar.

The Cessna taxied out to rising drums, turned and headed for the dark horizon. Two burning barrels marked the end of his runway. He cleared them and disappeared.

Then the drums seemed to stop. She turned to the *hounfor* and saw the people as they turned toward her. The dancers had slowed to the iron beat of the ogan. The *mambo* called to her softly.

"Madame." Fires burned before the ascending serpent.

The ceremony for John-Paul was called in Creole *wete mo danba dlo*. She had never heard it referred to in English. In French it was *retirer les morts d'en bas de l'eau*. Its purpose was to call back the souls of the dead from Guinee, bring them back safely to a place of honor and to the aid of the living. One side of the temple consisted of rows of painted, inlaid jars in the brightest colors, the *govi* that would contain the *ti bon ange* of the reclaimed dead. Lara thought of it as her last chance to address her brother's restless spirit, and through him to regain her own soul.

"Madame Lara."

Lara went across the field to the *hounfor,* passed between the fires and stood by the *poto mitan.* The *mambo* fixed her with a steady stare as though willing her to understand more than could be said. She spoke in a Creole so accented that Lara could hardly make it out, a language different from that which she spoke every Tuesday and Thursday in the market. One of the servants from the hotel translated for her.

"Only the rosary tonight. Mr. John-Paul he is not coming. Not this night."

"Why?" Lara asked, addressing herself to the *mambo.*

"You will ask him tomorrow. He will come tomorrow night."

"Is there trouble?"

The *mambo* kept her in the beam of that unbroken stare for a moment and then took Lara's hand.

"No trouble," the old servant said, although the *mambo* had not spoken. "A good rosary tonight. Tomorrow a good passage."

Roger drove them back to the family house on the shore, a few kilometers south of the hotel grounds.

"It happens," Roger told her as they drove through the scrub. "You know John-Paul. Always the contrarian. You'll have to pay for another *retirer les morts.*"

"Everything seemed right," Lara said.

Back at the house, Roger had a drink and Lara kept him company.

"Do you know more than you're telling me, Rog? If this was the date for it, why didn't they follow through?"

"Because it's dangerous."

"Why dangerous?"

"Dangerous to the *ti bon ange*. To John-Paul's soul." He seemed abstracted. He followed his rum with a second. "You know he has to be brought out of the sea. Out of Guinee. The soul is vulnerable in transit." He laughed and shook the ice in his drink.

"Why are you laughing, Roger?"

"I'm thinking of him there, Lara. I loved him. I'm not really laughing."

She watched him. He did seem to be laughing but she decided to take his word for it.

"The soul outside the body is always in danger," he told her. "Every religion says so. Now and at the hour of our death? The time of passage draws the enemies of the soul."

Lara thought of her own soul that must be out there as well, under the reef.

"Some Colombians are coming," Roger said. "I was really supposed to wait for their OK."

"I'm sure they'll approve."

Roger refilled his drink.

"They're sending down Hilda Bofil. A definite pain in the privates. Very contentious woman."

"Roger," Lara said, "I'm sorry we got in the way of all this. You understand why I had to come."

Roger looked at her for a long moment and finished his drink.

"Sure, baby." He stood up and kissed her and went outside to the car.

Out over the ocean, the first devil came with a change in the color of darkness. The swell of the mountains fell away and the phosphorescent glimmer of the inshore bay spread out beneath him. Ahead was the monochrome presentation of the sea, without forgiveness. A towering black cloud rose above the island, snake-shaped. When the engine began to cough, his instrument lights flickered. When they settled down, he saw the manifold gauge flat and dark.

A failure of information, Soto thought, unknown things. Beautiful machine, what troubles thee? The devil.

When he moved the throttle forward and felt the machine dying in his arms, he tried to put her in a turn. Proclaimed by the dead instruments, the plane was enfolded in ignorance, a random object awkwardly placed in the sky. And he was another random object, aloft and stripped of power, afloat in silence as in the old dream of flying. The bad one.

He thought: The water! If it had been left unguarded, contaminated! Water, such a simple thing. He closed his eyes and put his arm across his face.

Two shrimpers working between reefs saw him hit and go down fast. There had been the usual calm engine noise of an ascending plane, then silence, and out of the silent fall the crash, a great violence of sundered metal connections, hissing, steam, a series of whirlpools seeming to set each other off. Shrimp vanished. The fishermen would swear they felt the shear of the plane's wings.

After Roger left, she could not sleep. For one thing, the drums did not stop when the ceremony ended; the sound of the rosary in the distance shifted into Creole, singing honor to the gods.

Now that she had seen the temple at the lodge again, the *govi* jars in which spirits were conveyed, she could not get the pictures out of her mind. She thought of her own soul, larvalike, breathing to the undersea rhythms. To meet one's soul again, what would that be like? She imagined it as a judgment. I see myself in the mirror but my thoughts throw no reflection. My words cast no shadows, she thought. She imagined her present self as composed of two dimensions: an agent of influence, a professor of lies. Tomorrow she would be her former self, whoever that had been. Her eyes would change.

Suddenly she missed Michael. It had been folly to bring him but it was what she had wanted, that he see what would happen to her, that he be nearby. Then they would truly be bound. They would begin again. Because his situation was so like hers, the two of them together were no accident.

She began wandering naked through the rooms with a flashlight, then, hearing servants somewhere in the house, she put on a terrycloth robe. For a moment she thought she heard rain on the leaves outside, but it was only the wind rattling kapok branches against a metal roof.

She went along the second-floor patio hallway to John-Paul's room. The door was unlocked; she pushed it open and played her beam on the *vevers* painted on the walls and on the inlaid chests stacked on the floor. She moved the circle of light into the corners of the room. There were drawings she had not seen before, even woven *vevers* of gods she did not know. None of it had been there the last time she had seen his bedroom. It was as though someone had devised a secret wake in the room where he had died. Around the windows and on top of the framed pictures on the walls were branches of a plant she did not recognize, fragrant with a biting, musky smell.

Farther along, her beam fixed on glowing eyes. A man

crouched in one corner of the room. He looked excited, he smiled. Perhaps only guilty and surprised. When he stood up she recognized him as a man named Armand. He had been a boat builder and worked as a handyman at the *habitation*.

"Madame," he said, laughing.

She thought he seemed unsound. She had always known him to be a sensible man who was said to be a Jehovah's Witness.

"What's this?" she asked him, pointing to the strange *vevers*.

"*Bizango*," he said, his smile draining away.

It was a word one rarely heard, the name of a secret society to which John-Paul was said to belong. People feared it. She wondered if her soul in Marinette's custody had any connection with *bizango*.

"But Armand. You didn't put these here?"

"No, madame," the old man said.

Outside, a vehicle pulled up in front of the house. She went to the balcony rail and shone her light behind the headlights. Roger Hyde was driving one of the camouflage jeeps from the lodge. There were two white men in the rear seat, in uniforms that matched the jeep's coloration. She thought they must be Colombian *milicianos*. They did not care to be illuminated; they shouted at her until she moved the beam away. One pointed his weapon. She shut off the light and heard Roger coming up the outside stairway, moving more quickly than was his custom.

"Lara?"

"I'm here, Roger. What's wrong?"

He took her hand.

"Be cool, sweetheart. We lost the plane. It went down over the reef."

"Oh my God. Oh Roger." She put a hand to her face. "And the pilot?"

"The pilot bought it, poor guy," Roger said. "And poor us because the Colombians are here from Rodney. They're not happy."

"But they can't blame us."

Roger smiled unhappily. "They have to blame someone, Lara."

"Do we have to go to the lodge?"

"They want us at the lodge. It's going to be difficult. The woman they sent is very" — he shrugged — "difficult." He was more upset than she ever remembered him being.

While they were driving to the lodge, veering onto the shoulder, dodging holes in the road, dodging the talus around them, she asked, "Roger, you must tell me about *bizango*."

He made a noise like laughter. "There may come a time I'll do that, baby. Not now."

"You're scaring me."

"You haven't done anything wrong to anyone," Roger said. "Remember that."

That could not be true, she thought. She was not reassured.

14

THE FACTOR was a yellowing man in a blue plaid shirt who sat behind a counter near the street entrance to a disorderly shop of some sort. The place had a sharp smell of tobacco and of a bitter liquor that stung the eyes. A second door at the back led to a courtyard where men were offloading sacks from a battered truck.

Michael introduced himself.

"How did you travel?" the rusty-looking man asked him.

"On the bus," Michael told him.

"Yes?"

"Oh," Michael added. "To the east." That was the formula by which he understood Masons recognized each other in Fort Salines. He thought it might apply. "Yep. Eastward. To the east."

It was apparent the yellowing man understood nothing of what Michael was trying to convey. Nevertheless he presented a card that declared him to be Edouard Ashraf.

"Was it beautiful?" he asked. "No? Aha." He seemed pleased. "From the capital? No one comes that way."

"It was all right," Michael said. "Of course I was stuck there all day and half the night."

The Factor looked genuinely sympathetic.

The bus had left him in darkness a few minutes before dawn. His night ride had been fraught with Creole whispers, laughter that included him out. Then, on his arrival, a market had assembled around him in the sudden morning light of the northern city. The sea was nearby, a joyous dazzle. The mountain range over which he had come erupted from deep green shadow. He had been dreading day, the prospect of standing alone there, tropical sun lighting the blood guilt of his skin. But then it had seemed all right.

Factor Ashraf's yellowness was unsettling. Whatever jaundice he harbored had spread over his eyes, soaked the whites and stained his eyeballs. His skin appeared the color of lined foolscap. Together with the shock of blondish hair that rose mysteriously from his lemon scalp like a wick, it made him look to Michael like a wax *santo*. It was all, he assured himself, his fatigue, hypnagogic hallucinatory impressions. But the vertigo he could not shake off was a kind of sensory infection. As though there were really some rough magic everywhere.

"I was told you could direct me to the Bay of Saints Hotel," Michael said. Cautiously, he glanced around but the little shop was empty. On the dusty shelves, packages wrapped in twine were stacked beside medicine bottles that looked a century old. The bottles contained liquids that ranged in color from water-clear to factor-colored saffron to amber.

"I thought it was a different man. An American."

"Well," Michael said, "that's me."

"You're Michael?"

"Yes. Michael."

"You have to be careful," the Factor told him.

"Yes," Michael said. "Have you seen my friend?"

"It's unsafe," said the Factor, ignoring his question. "On certain days it is unwise to leave the city. Beware after dark. Avoid the poorest districts." He spoke as if by rote.

"I understand," Michael said. "I'll be careful."

"Maybe your soldiers will help you."

"Really," Michael said, "I hope it doesn't come to that."

He promptly told Michael the way to his hotel. It was, he said, within walking distance and could be safely walked.

In the market there were butchered dogfish for sale along with barrels of squirming creatures, living tangles of antennae and tentacles among bloody chopped shell. Cockles and mussels, cones and mandibles and trilobites. Everything was wet, slick, bright, stinking and attended by flies. Women wielding box cutters opened crates full of electrical batteries, spools of thread. Little groups of children wandered from stall to stall, unsmiling and silent. Only a few begged listlessly.

"Money," they murmured softly. *"Lajan, blan."*

He handed out the small crumbling bills he had acquired for his nocturnal nightmare passage through the army roadblock. In the dead of night, small stick-thin boys with gleaming eyes had led him from shack to shack where slumberous officials examined his passport by kerosene lamp, stamped it, variously laughed or scowled at him, beleaguered him with incomprehensible questions he foolishly struggled to answer.

"Lajan, blan," wailed the market children in their beggars' patois.

He made his way to the sea, as he had been advised. The streets were poor, of a poverty underlaid with some destroyed elegance. There were thick-walled houses in the

Spanish style and wrought-iron balconies hung with laundry. Teenagers in spotless school uniforms giggled charitably at him and said hello, *bonjour,* and did not beg. The ache of forlorn hope, the young. Some of the children were about his son's age.

With the ocean on his right, he headed for the western end of town, the part they called the Carenage. The breezes carried a heavy scent of oranges. An orange liqueur, he had read, was manufactured there.

Sky and ocean together were an overwhelming brightness. With each shift of the wind he caught sour rot from the tide line under the seawall and then the irresistible orange sweetness. Everything dazzled. More uniformed children passed and one long-legged coltish kid halted her friends and came across the empty littered street to him.

"*M'sieu,*" she said. "*Une plim? Souple, m'sieu'.*"

Michael stopped and stared at her.

"*Souple, m'sieu. Une plim.* Give me a pen, if you please, sah."

Michael went through his pockets, jammed with travel detritus: credit card receipts, seat checks, ticket stubs, crumpled bills. Somewhere there was a ballpoint pen. Light hurt his eyes. Sweet laughter. He was the privileged comedian. He gave her the pen he had used to scrawl forms at the military roadblocks. The island governance, however revolutionary, believed in forms. Moving on, he patted himself down for his passport for the tenth time.

He followed the oceanfront boulevard to a cliff overlooking the town. The road forked, one route snaking around the bare rock face to follow the shore and the other curving into a cul-de-sac from which a flight of cement steps disappeared into a wall of creepers and cactus.

Michael climbed the steps and found himself in a garden

beside a swimming pool. There was a view across the bay, and atop the Morne on the far side stood the grim bones of a Spanish citadel, recognizable from photographs. There was an outdoor bar adjoining the pool, where a tall man in a light suit and dark sport shirt stood watching Michael recover his breath from the climb.

"Hi," Michael said to him. The man nodded. He was, or once had been, Hollywood handsome in something of a 1940s style. He had a graying black mustache and fine tanned skin and large, expressive eyes. An actor's eyes.

A hotel servant sauntered out to take Michael's backpack. No one asked him to register. Taken to a room with a view of the ocean, he gave the porter a dollar and settled down against the pillows.

Very shortly there was a knock on his door. He rose stiffly and buttoned his shirt. When he opened the door he found the man he had seen at the bar. The man seemed to be looking over his shoulder to see if they were being observed.

"Welcome to St. Trinity," the man said. "Michael?"

Michael relaxed and extended his hand.

"Let me properly greet you, Michael," the man said. "I'm Roger Hyde."

"I've heard of you."

"Good things I hope?"

"Yes," Michael said, "of course." The man seemed genuinely hopeful that what she had said of him were good things.

"Lara sends her best."

"Great," Michael said. "Where is she?"

"I have to tell you, Michael, that we've had some major difficulties in our operations. What with the war."

"Of course," Michael said.

"Things have got rather tough."

"Oh, no," Michael exclaimed. A foolish utterance, he realized. He felt a first thrill of panic.

"We've got to sort it out. Lara and I. She'll explain when she comes."

"When will that be?"

Roger smiled, a bit like a hotelier with hospitality problems. "As soon as she can make it."

"Can I reach her?"

Roger shook his head. "The war. She'll explain. I know you're a good friend to Lara. But this is local stuff, you might say. Meanwhile, you're our guest. Drinks on the house. Everything." He was extremely tense but very controlled. "I'll tell the desk."

"Great," said Michael. "Thank you."

"Mrs. Robert will be at the desk if you need anything." He started out the door and paused. "You're not going out? I mean, away from the hotel?"

"I was going to wait for Lara."

"That's the best plan," Roger repeated. "If you go out — we don't like dull colors here — wear something a little red, and keep smiling. OK?"

"OK," Michael said. "Why?"

Roger had what looked like a necktie in his hand, which he proffered. He ignored the question.

"You might wrap it around your head. If you leave the hotel tonight. Got it?"

"Well, yes."

"Sort of a special holiday. Do you have lots of small change? Small bills? Good. We'll contact Lara for you, OK?"

"I understand," Michael said. "Thank you."

The necktie was small and scarlet-colored; it reminded

him of a boy's confirmation tie. It was wrinkled like a small boy's possession. He had bought one for his own son not too long ago.

He was at the manageable edge of fear and he wanted Lara with him. He walked up and down in the room for a while until the linen cushions on the big metal-framed bed were too much for him. He lay down exhausted, battered senseless by the bus's motion, and slept.

When he awakened the sun was low over the western quarter of the bay. Immediately he picked up the room phone in slim hope of a message. The phone seemed not to be working. He had a shower and brushed his teeth, for which even the most strenuous-minded guidebooks suggested bottled water. The trip had been difficult but exhilarating and he felt better. The thought that he would see her, that he had broken free into a different life, set his heart racing. He realized he was hungry.

Outside, the declining sun cast light like a bright October afternoon. The few clouds looked high and dry. A waiter was stacking candles at one of the poolside tables. Michael went to the hotel desk where a very old lady with a fin-de-siècle ivory fan told him he had no messages. The old lady, he thought, vaguely resembled Lara.

He sat down at a table, ordered a rum drink and was immediately joined by a man, a *blan* in an open aloha shirt and flip-flops. The man sat heavily, directly across from him.

"Van Dreele," announced the heavy man. "With an NGO, are you? American? Canadian?"

"My name is Michael," Ahearn told him. "I don't work for an organization, not here. I came to look around. And to look at paintings. It's my first time."

"Oof," said the Dutchman, as though he had been poked firmly in the stomach. "How was the trip from the airport? The roads are clear?"

"I don't know," Michael said. "I came from Rodney. By bus. The roads were in pretty bad shape."

Van Dreele gaped at him in silence. When the *plat du jour* arrived — it was crevettes — they both ate greedily. Occasionally Van Dreele would look up from his dinner to stare at Michael.

"I was here last September for the first round of the elections. They thought they could scare me away this time. But not me," said the old Dutchman in triumph. He wiped the sauce delicately from his mustache. "I gave them a hard time."

"And were the elections fair?" Michael asked.

"Well, the Americans' favorites won," Van Dreele said. "Their new favorites. The new improved army." He looked up and saw a young woman coming up the stone steps into the restaurant. "Here's the person to ask."

He introduced Michael to a magazine journalist named Liz McKie.

"What brings you here, Michael?" she asked. "At a time like this. You writing?"

"No, just diving."

McKie assumed an expression of puzzled interest. "Say what?"

"I'm here for the beach."

"No shit?" the reporter said. "The beach, huh?"

Van Dreele laughed darkly.

"Well," Michael told them, "I thought I'd look at the native art, too. Buy some pictures."

"Hey, Dirk," she said to Van Dreele, "I know you're

avoiding me. Give me a break this time. What is the story on this guy, Dirk?" she asked. "Is he a spook? I mean, he doesn't look like a . . ." Whatever she had been about to say went unsaid.

"Maybe he's here to buy the hotel," suggested Van Dreele. "It's being sold."

They heard trucks pulling up outside. A party of local soldiery tramped up from the road. Mrs. Robert ran out to meet them.

"Hey, you boys," she shouted at them. "You can't come in here." The three soldiers who had come laughed at her but stopped. A tall striking officer in British-style rig came up behind them; he was laughing too. Liz McKie walked over to him. Their handshake was affectionate. Then the officer and the three soldiers went back into the night. More trucks pulled up.

"They're after me," Van Dreele said. He did not seem to be joking. "Every time they miscount a vote I catch them. They want me out of here."

"I think they're surrounding the hotel."

"But it's being sold right now," Michael said.

"Are you here to buy it?" Liz McKie asked. "Along with the local art?" Still addressing Michael, she turned to perform for Van Dreele. "Gonna run it on the up-and-up? I hope Roger's staying on as manager. Where is old Rog anyhow?"

"He's at the lodge with Lara," Van Dreele said. "I guess they're stamping the papers."

"You wouldn't be down here with Lara?" Liz McKie asked. "Like, are you a friend of hers? One of her *tonton macoutes?*"

One of the old waiters came to the table to tell Michael

that there was a message for him. He excused himself and went to the desk. Mrs. Robert had the message, apparently brought on foot by a little boy who stood expectantly by. The message was from Roger Hyde. Miss Purcell was in conference, and the conference might last the night. Michael gave the boy one of his folded bills, to the great excitement of the child, and said good night to the people at his table and went back to his room.

Lying there, he could hear orders crooned in a mixture of British and American inflections. Running soldiers, the slap of their weapons, laughter. He heard the sea. But louder and louder, from how far away he could not tell, he heard drums. The hills behind the town made them echo and confused their direction.

Concentrating on them, he tried to unravel the rhythms and count the number of drums. There were too many — so many, he thought, that it was impossible to imagine the drummers at their devotions. The voices in the drums were as good as infinite with their turns and shadows, doubling and tripling and repeating and commenting on their own tattoos. Covering each other, featuring the premonition of a beat, the beat itself, its echo. Each pattern sounded of inevitability, so that what had to come next came, obvious only after the fact, surprising. Then repeated, it surprised again. If you followed a line of the beat you would know what you were about to hear and then hear it and have it repeated for you, each rendering ever so slightly different from the last. The drums made patterns that filled the mind's eye to capacity, crowded out the mind of the listener.

It occurred to him that if he opened himself to the drums he might find himself anywhere at all. He might be emptied of himself, turned into a shifting of the sand at the bottom of the sea outside his window. The drums were in nature, he thought, as surely as a bird call and its answer. They came from a place where the human touched everything else in the world, a secret crossing where they could draw spirits out of the dark.

When he dozed, he thought it must be the malaria pills he had taken, that he was hearing the drums in dreams. But when he stood up and drank from his bottled water or from the bottle of duty-free rum he had put beside the bed, he realized that they would always be there, they were incessant. Events he could not conceive were taking place within them, a different kind of time unraveling. They sounded counterpoint with the sea, who kept her own time.

He was in the grip of some peculiar lust, erect and alone, as though he were waiting in vain for a woman he had lost rather than one found, a woman whose features were melting away into forms he put out of his mind. He leaned into the drums, actually felt like dancing, and did dance, a freak dancing a solitary fever dance, aroused and terrified in his ratty hotel room by the city sea, throwing his arms about. He made himself stop, but it was hard to work free of the drums. In their many voices he heard his name.

Lara. Some of his dreams were of her. Some of Kristin. His skin felt tight with fever. The drums took him to the balcony, which overlooked the Carenage and the sea.

No escape in sleep; he kept going back to look at the ocean, the drums took him. Its surface was blank, there was no moon. But, he thought, there had been one the night before. In some other world. The drums never stopped, nor his wrestling with dreams. The ocean outside his window now had a quality he did not care for. Its darkness only concealed. Trying to pick out the reef line in faint starlight, he wondered where along its edge their dive would be. The place had so much ruin and bad history for an ocean to cover. Hateful angry gods one never suspected might command dimensions out there, gods who owed nothing to him or to reason. He felt more lonely than he had ever felt in his life.

15

THERE WERE NO messages for him at the desk the following day and no one seemed to know of a way he could contact Lara. He spent the morning walking along the Carenage, looking through the markets, declining to buy basketry, dispensing pens to the schoolchildren. Fishing boats with tortuously repaired rigging stood moored bow-landward where the Carenage ended, though it was hard, looking at them, to tell what kind of fish they followed. One had the dried carcass of a sea turtle stretched across its open forward hatch. All of them were brightly painted in the Haitian manner, named in Creole and sanctified with the portraits of saints and the designs that he would come to know as *vevers*, designs that signified the gods of the Haitian pantheon, whom the Christian saints also represented. The ancestors of the people at that end of the island, he had read, had come or been brought from Haiti after the revolution there.

At the edge of town, he walked unaware into an encampment of soldiers. Their uniforms were of a different shade than those of the soldiers he had seen around the hotel and their helmets had an unfamiliar shape. The men stared at him in hostile silence. Their rifles, stacked in the old infantry manner in the center of their bivouac, looked like relics. Some of them he thought might be M-1's of World War II manufacture. Two of the soldiers came toward him but were called back by a noncom in a language that Michael knew must be English but could not understand. As unconcernedly as possible, he reversed direction.

When the sun became too much for him he went back to the hotel. Still there was nothing from Lara. He put a bathing suit on and paddled among the frangipani blossoms in the pool, then lay down in his room for a while. Late in the afternoon he dressed and went outside. There were several soldiers sitting at the patio tables, officers of the island republic's new army, all in fresh camouflage fatigues and wearing sidearms. Soldiers in the same colors stood guard at the steps that led down to the road and on the rise behind the swimming pool that overlooked the bay.

Van Dreele was at the table closest to the hotel desk. Liz McKie sat with a tall, olive-skinned army officer whose trimmed military mustache and slightly hooded eyes made him at once noticeable and attractive. He looked thoughtful and most observant, and Liz McKie dwelled on his features with admiration.

Michael sat down at Van Dreele's table and ordered a beer.

"Enjoying yourself?" the Dutchman asked him.

Michael shrugged.

"Been to town?"

"I walked to the far edge of town."

"You saw the junta's army."

"Yes," Michael said. "I'm woefully uninformed."

Van Dreele had two newspapers, one Dutch, the other a *Miami Herald.* He gave Michael the *Herald,* and Michael tried to focus on it. The State Department said it was determined to support the new government, that the election might have been flawed but the junta had plainly lost, and it hoped the junta's army would stand down without bloodshed.

"So will the junta's army stand down?" he asked Van Dreele.

"Depends what you mean by stand down. They'll all go home when no one gives them dinner. But then we'll all have to get through the night."

From the far table by the pool, McKie called to him.

"Hey, Michael! Let's see your *El Heraldo.*"

Van Dreele relinquished his newspaper with a gesture and Michael brought it over to the table where McKie was sitting with her officer friend.

"Sit down, Michael," she said. She introduced the officer, Colonel Junot, and took the paper.

"Nothing about you, Boonsie," she told her friend.

"Keeping a low profile," he told Michael with a wink. "I am the stealth candidate, slowly slowly slowly sneaking behind the throne." He made a weasel of his hand and slinked it across the table. He wore a Rolex. "Anyhow," he told McKie, "I'm giving you exclusives. I'm gonna appear dramatically in your eyewitness accounts. Amazing America!"

"Not too dramatically, OK? And," she said, "I think we should call my accounts firsthand instead of eyewitness. Eyewitness suggests you've seen something awful. Right, Mike?"

Michael agreed.

"How was the beach?" she asked.

"What?"

"The beach. *La playa. La plage.* That's what you came for, right? The beach?"

"Yes," he said. "But I went for a walk."

"Really, where?" she asked.

"To the edge of town."

"See any American troops?"

"American troops? No."

McKie and Colonel Junot exchanged a look. Then Junot shrugged. "Supposed to be a medical unit at Dajubon. And some Special Ops. They're on our side."

"Yeah," McKie said, "you sure of that, Boonsie?"

"Sure and certain. America forever. You're looking at a veteran of Operation Urgent Fury." He looked at Michael, challenging him. "Never heard of it?"

Michael had heard of it. "The Grenada invasion."

"As a young shavetail, as they say at Fort Benning. Sub-altern. I think we came in handy."

"The operation where the navy bombed the madhouse," McKie reminded them. "Friendly fire."

No one said anything for a moment.

"Oh," she said, "listen. Drums. And it's broad daylight."

"*Retirer,*" the colonel told her. "For John-Paul Purcell. *Retirer les morts d'en bas de l'eau.*"

McKie spoke as though she were correcting him. "*Wete mo danba dlo.*"

"Very good," the colonel said. "You're becoming very accomplished, Liz."

Michael, too, listened to the drums.

"So how many you think there are, Mike?" Liz McKie asked him.

"I don't know," he said.

"Four," she told him. She looked impudently at Junot, displaying her knowledge.

"Only four?" Michael asked.

She laid her right hand on the rusting metal tabletop and peeled the drums from her long graceful fingers.

"Four drums," she explained, "for the rites of *rada*. What you might call the brass is a piece of iron, an ogan." She winked at him. "Listen, Michael!" Her open, long-toothed face looked perfectly happy. "The *petite*. The *seconde*. And *maman*, the big one. Can you hear them?"

"Yes."

"Aren't they good?"

"Yes," he said, "they're good."

"Bigger than us," the colonel said. "Bigger than all of us."

Michael let them buy him drinks until he was dazed again. The prospect of his own room, its drum-haunted silence and darkness and unreassuring light, frightened him. The whole world of otherness was waiting for him there, called up out of the ocean by drums. It was no place for him.

When he went in and turned on the bed lamp, Lara was waiting there for him.

"Michael." She looked pale and tired. "Don't be frightened. Not of me."

His instinct was to hold her and in the next moment he went against her, gathered her up out of the drums. She had been made to be like him and familiar, her swellings and smells — the French soap, her breath, pleasant as a troubadour might claim some little virgin's might be. But she was breathless; she raised her throat from his hands to speak. He was smothering her.

"Oh God, Michael," she said. "You're . . ." She shook her head and her loose hair, laughed and touched his erection. "You're all engage," she said, in neither English nor French.

"Engage. Engaged."

"Are we engaged, then?"

"Sure," he said, "we're a couple of fiancées."

She sat him down on the bed and leaned into his shoulder. He could not see her face.

"What I have to say is not so good, eh?"

He stroked her glistening hair. He almost laughed at the sad fatefulness with which she spoke. What she had said, he had expected. Maybe telegraphed in the drums, why not?

"I was followed here. Someone is waiting for me to come out. If I don't come out they'll come for me."

For one brief moment he felt humiliated, a mark, the soft center of a gypsy switch, the Murphy game.

"Someone is waiting for you?" he asked lightly. "I thought you owned the hotel. I thought you were with me."

He pushed her back so that they could lie down together. He felt her relax beside him.

"I wish it were a joke," she said. "I lost something I was responsible for. A man's been killed."

He thought about this and said, "You told me no drugs."

"That's what they told me," she said. "Honestly."

"Oh shit," he said.

"They are South Americans," she said. "John-Paul and Roger worked with them and maybe there were drugs."

He laughed unhappily. She sat up.

"Will you not treat me like a criminal? As though I schemed?"

"I think you schemed. I have to think that, understand? Otherwise I'll feel like a total idiot."

"Oh, my dear Michael," she said. "You have to believe me." She was pressed against him. "My scheme was not to hurt anyone, I swear. A worst case happened."

"I keep looking at that door," Michael said. "I keep thinking of your escort."

"They won't come yet," she said.

"What do I have to do, Lara?"

"You have to remember that I really love you. I know what love is, I'm not some crazy person. Maybe someday I'll stop but now I do."

"That's easy," Michael said. "What else?"

"You have to dive a wreck. You have to get three cases out of the aft compartment of a Cessna 185."

He sat silently until he could manage a wan uncalled-for joke. "Cocaine? Can I have some?"

She looked really terrified then.

"To the best of my knowledge," she said, "it is not drugs. I packed some emeralds and some old drawings that may be valuable. It's true the emeralds are being smuggled. I don't care, do you?"

"I'm not sure I have the skills, Lara."

"You dive wrecks in Lake Superior every summer. You can do it."

"Is the pilot in the plane?"

She shrugged. A shrug of sympathy that seemed genuine.

"What if I fuck it up?"

"It's not drugs, remember."

"What if I fuck it up?"

"They'll blame me. And you'll be in danger. You might have to run to the Americans. What can you tell them?"

"I'm not good at running. I thought you were an American citizen."

"I am. But they won't . . . you know. I'm involved through my family. They won't let me go. Unless I get them the cargo back."

Then she told him more than he wanted to hear. She and Roger had panicked because of the coup. They thought the lodge would be raided; they sent the plane off without checking with them. The South Americans. She was preoccupied with some ceremony involving her brother's soul.

"I don't think we have a chance," Michael said. "I don't know much about this, but that's my feeling. Mind if I ask you an impolite question?"

She blew him an imaginary bubble of impatience, in the French manner.

"You're a diver," he said. "You're very able. Why don't you dive it?"

"I've never done a night dive."

"Can that be true?"

"Never. Or a wreck. I go for the reefs, Michael. For the trip down the wall. God, don't you think I would if I could?"

This is where I have placed myself, he thought. If he did not panic, imagine tortures, if he accepted the consequences of his actions, if he was strong, he might imagine himself a lucky man. The most beautiful woman he had ever seen was cowering on his bed, demanding heroic measures. Life had gone that way. He thought of the man with the wheelbarrow. He listened to the drums.

"If we fail," she said, "we can die together. I can see to that." She might have been reading his thoughts. Yours in the ranks of death. "But I think it's an easy dive."

Undressing her, taking up her tense body, he felt like killing her then and there. Returning the perfect form to the entropy that composed it, sending it back through the drums.

She said "I love you," the old song, but it made him feel: Here is a companion in danger. Us against the wall. Here is a friend in an adventure. This, he thought, and clung to the thought, is where the drums had taken him, to a world other than middle-aged marriage and professorship and the tiny world of Fort Salines. He had never been a coward. Without physical courage, he had once told a couple of his colleagues, there is no moral courage. A couple of his colleagues who didn't want to hear it.

Unsheathing her, taking her up like a drink. He turned her over on her belly and said, "Let's see."

She said, "What?"

He had meant, Let's see in all the spaces of these bodies together on the edge, by the floating yellow cans that marked oblivion, headed down the wall, let's see if we can find what the other side of the drums is made of. Let's see if there are dark poison flowers in your cunt, if my finger on that little curiosity where love has pitched his mansion tonight produces visions to terrify.

"Let's see," he said.

When he made her come he could hear the language of everything created beyond his understanding.

Afterward he swigged the rum and offered her some. She was weeping, refusing to let his prick go down, a little comic pursuit like a kid worrying a balloon.

"Tell again," he said, "about the bottom of the sea." He asked because he had a notion that it was in some fashion where he was headed.

"Guinee," she said. "Because the slaves believed that by jumping overboard they returned to Africa. So it's where the soul goes for a while. Guinee, it's very beautiful there."

"So maybe we'll go there."

"We'll go there. John-Paul is there. My soul is there sometimes." Then she said, "It's not always beautiful. They're lonely there."

Someone knocked on the door. The knock was so soft as to seem childlike. They were scarcely sure they had heard it, yet it was there. Her eyes opened wide with fear, a look into the heart of the drums.

"They want me."

"Lara."

She nestled against him and said something he could not hear.

"Don't lie to me," he said. "I'm going to give you everything."

"No, never. On my soul." She smiled a little and moved away. "When I have one."

16

THE HOTEL'S dive shop was a few kilometers past town, along the beach. Soldiers were smoking in the palm grove behind it. Michael and Roger Hyde went in quietly and turned on the light, waiting to see if anyone noticed them, but no one did. Several minutes later an islander who worked at the shop appeared in the company of two tiny children, who commenced an evening ramble of the premises. In all but one regard they played like children anywhere. Stalking each other above the bins and storage racks, they whispered in patois.

The shop was not large. It was plainly sinking into a state of abandonment that would render its equipment useless before too long. It had a single high-pressure, low-volume compressor with an electric motor on its own generator. Parts were in need of lubrication. While Roger watched, Michael and the bare-chested Trinitejan, whose name was Hippolyte, worked on the gear. They got some linseed oil and rubber washers, checked the valves and rinsed salt off the masks. The Trinitejan soldiers had gone back to the road.

The tanks and regulators looked serviceable enough and the compressor seemed to draw its source air from the coconut grove outside the shop. Michael had once begun a dive in Baja where the compressor that filled the tanks was located in a service station. The air it supplied was liberally laced with the fumes of economy Pemex leaded, and a few minutes of down time provided an effect similar to the consumption of death cap toadstool. This Trinitejan outfit, by contrast, had been pretty safety-minded. According to Roger, a husband and wife from Martinique had run it. They had stayed on well into the major troubles and were only a few weeks gone.

"Looks like it was a busy shop," Michael said to his new friends.

"In the old days it was," Roger declared. "Really was."

Michael took one of the 80-cubic-foot cylinders and tried applying it directly to the compressor. He had only worked with portable machines before but the join seemed to work. He pumped the tank to something under 3,000 psi, screwed on the regulator and took a lungful. It seemed sweet enough. The taste of the air in the mouthpiece gave him a charge of anticipation, the thrill of game time. He tried the tank again.

"It's a beautiful reef offshore," Roger said. "They call it Petite Afrique because of the shape." He formed the curves of Africa with his hands, swelling breast and scimitar horn. "Two miles out."

"Is that where we're going?"

"We're going farther. To the ledge."

"How deep is the thing?"

"We don't know." He turned to the Trinitejan. "Hippolyte thinks he knows where the plane went down. He says you can see it down there. From the surface you can kind of make it out."

"Should be able to see the operating lights," Michael said with a shiver. "I presume the pilot's still down there?"

No one answered him. The shop employed old-style French-made auxiliary tanks that could be fitted to the diver's main cylinder. They engaged with the shift of a J-valve and Michael disliked using them. When you ran low on air with one attached, the supply in your main tank simply stopped cold. If blind groping over your shoulder failed to locate the valve, you went airless, an absolute condition. Nevertheless, he fitted one on. Frightened, out of practice, he knew he would overbreathe, use up his air in little more than half an hour. He filled two other tanks; it was heavy work and he was sweating, exhausted. It was getting late and he had not had a proper sleep in a long time. A false dawn seemed to rise across the bay from the Morne.

"The accident's been reported," Roger said. "Presumably the U.S. Coast Guard in the Mona Passage picked it up. Or the British in Grand Turk. But the Trinitejans have no helicopter operative we know about and they shouldn't have the location."

"A lot of people could have seen him fall," Michael said.

"That's right," Roger said. "That's why we have to move fast."

Michael carried his gear and a wetsuit down to the hotel's dive boat. Hippolyte had to fill the boat's engine with fuel. He himself brought along a mask and snorkel.

They got the tanks into the dive boat and poled the boat over the inshore reef. Even in darkness the bank of dead coral was visible below, a chalky mass catching the glow of the night sky. At the edge of the reef they shoved off into breaking surf. The seas were manageable, slowed by the outer barrier. Still they had to hold fast. The tanks, secured along the inboard rail, rattled together like conspirators.

Beyond the break, Roger started up the engine, giving the boat enough throttle to hold its place. Michael sat in the small cabin, in a folding chair with his back to the bulkhead. Hippolyte was muttering little songs, jesting rhymes and ditties. He seemed anything but tense as he studied a chart in the rusty dream of his muffled flashlight. The boat was running without lights and Michael thought he had the sense of other unlit boats around them.

"I've survived a couple of these," Roger told Michael. "Glad I didn't ride shotgun on this one."

"Who was the pilot?" Michael asked.

"Colombian," Roger said. "Lara rode down from Puerto Rico with him."

"She did?" That might have been the first time he thought about her fine raptures over the diving. Why should she think it was an easy dive? Unless something was laid out there for him to retrieve. These things went down. He read the papers as much as anyone else. Actually he read them less. But sufficiently. In any case, he was going to do it. Hers in the ranks of death.

While Roger read the island's offshore charts, Michael put on the lower part of his wetsuit over his shorts. They were large, top and bottom. He would have to be careful to get the air out of the suit before going down. Otherwise it might mean shooting to the surface on the way up, filling his lungs with his own death's blood.

Hippolyte spoke up. *"La lune! Regardez!"*

And there she was, a warp short of full, risen over the Morne. It lit up the bay far more effectively than the old town's unsteady municipal flickerings.

"Take the glasses and have a look around," Roger told Michael. "See if we have any privacy."

Michael scanned the horizon line. The binoculars were fancy strap-on navy night-vision items that turned the dark seascape into a digital optic entertainment. No vessels appeared, no one. Dead ahead, the edge of ocean was broken by two tangled shapes, mangrove cays whose leaves, weirdly tinted in the night glasses, shuddered on the wind.

"Nothing."

Roger and Hippolyte were talking earnestly in Creole, Hippolyte pointing from the cays to the hulk of the mountain.

"He thinks if we follow the reef from Sauvequipeut toward Haut Morne we'll go over it."

"How can he tell in the dark?" Michael asked.

"There should be an oil slick when we get there. And it's not as dark to him as it is to you. He's a shrimper."

"A shrimper?"

"He knows the bottom very well. It's his house. He's counting off the little mangrove islands," Roger told Michael. He himself opened the throttle and they chugged along at a deliberate speed. After a few minutes Hippolyte asked for a cigarette. He took it and leaned forward to let Roger light it for him.

"He figures distance by smokes," Roger told Michael.

They followed the reef line, Hippolyte keeping the field glasses focused on the two mangrove cays across a spur of reef. In a while, he requested another cigarette. The swell increased. Finally he tossed the stub of his Marlboro overboard and said, *"C'est là."*

"Oop!" Roger quickly came about.

He held the bow to the wind with one arm. Hippolyte and Michael hurried to the port rail. Hippolyte leaned down with the viewing glass he used for spotting sponges, a four-sided wooden box with a window at the end. Roger peered into the box with the night glasses. He muttered something and passed them to Michael.

They were over the wall. Using the binoculars and Hippolyte's contraption it was possible to see the higher ledges, patterns of elkhorn and tube coral descending into red and gray murk. A few gas cans and fan belts littered the highest shelf.

"What's he seeing?" Michael asked.

Hippolyte was looking across the reef toward the mountain range.

"*C'est là,*" he told them. "*Voilà isir. Ici.*"

They tried using the hand light in his viewing box but saw no more at first than the outline of their own anxious faces.

Michael took the box and, with Roger and Hippolyte holding him, had a long look down the slope. After a minute or so he thought he saw a faint green glow. In a little time, the glow doubled. Trick of the eye? The points shifted, fluttered, blinked in his bleary vision, but they were light and they were constant. There was a little red light as well.

"I think it might be an instrument panel. It's deep."

"Well," Roger said after a moment, "let's get it, brother."

They went below to a cramped cabin with a non-functioning compressor and some empty tank racks. Michael fixed a regulator to the tank and tested it.

"So what's down there, Roger?"

Roger had a photograph of an airplane. He showed it to Michael under a cabin light.

"This is a Cessna 185. Two seats up front, a single seat behind it. Behind the single seat is a four-and-a-half-by-five storage compartment. It contains two watertight cases weighing about ten pounds each. Also a metal tube of drawings and paintings. Get the paintings if you can. But the two cases are the thing."

"I thought it was always packaged to float?"

"What can I say?" Roger asked him. "Rash optimism."

Michael took his fins and went on deck. Roger came up behind him.

"I don't know your temperament, Mike. You might find some upsetting things that you should just, ah, leave alone."

"Like what?"

"Like the pilot."

"Oh."

"He was a very determined guy," Roger explained. "Nice fella."

"You knew him?"

"Oh," Roger said, "I knew them all to talk to. Some of them were charming."

Just then, at the far end of the bay, a high-speed helicopter made the crossing from Point aux Riches to Mont Cesar. It moved in a circuit of whirling lights.

"Shit," Michael said. The helicopter probably indicated the American presence in one of its aspects.

Roger took him by the arm. "Wear your salutation. Wear it for Erzule. And for Lara." He tied the red band around Michael's forehead over the mask.

Michael was looking at the helicopter.

"Go, Michael," Roger said. "Never mind them. Go. Go." He put his palm against the red band. "*Ave Maria Purísima*. Go, for Christ's sake."

Michael, to his own considerable surprise, made the sign of the cross and fell backward into the darkness.

He had taken a hand light. For a while he treaded water, squeezing air from his oversized buoyancy compensator. Then he let himself slowly descend, sweeping the top of the wall with his light. There, it was eel grass and fans, litter, beer cans and wrenches, bristling with spiny urchins. There was a good deal of chalk, dead elkhorn. Hardly any fish, a few tangs. More or less what he had expected.

The little fever, the sick sting of fear in the gullet he had been breathing through all day, eased a little as he went down. It helped, performing the nice necessities of diving, to become a different animal in a different element. The wonder of it appeased his imagination.

He felt himself landing lightly on the next ledge; his fins touched, then his knees. He disengaged, turned over on his back and twisted upright. Brain coral here and a kerosene can. He checked his depth gauge. Eight meters, twenty-six feet.

Crossing the ledge over the elkhorn, an admiring barracuda came to share the dive, then, quicker than the eye, a second appeared in the beam of his light. When he was on the wall, descending again, they followed him down in a slow spiral.

Equalizing, he felt as though the pressure against his body were the weight of darkness itself. Dark possibility above and below, everywhere beyond the little circle of his light. But close at hand, the wall was richer than he had imagined. Colors came forward almost violently, flashed into life within the vagrant cordon he spread. Star coral hung on the underledges; there were caves where baby sponges grew on a gleaming black carpet, like anemones in a lava field. Black coral, something rare. Probing farther along, he saw that a lot of it had been chipped away; the claw of a lost hammer glinted among the fans.

Attended by the 'cudas and a cautious trumpet fish, he moved out from the face and tried to accelerate a little, to lose more of the air in the big BC. He passed beautiful terraces of brain coral. When he had first seen brain, diving years before, it had stirred his faith, the form of it, suggesting in that deep liquid world the mind itself, the mind of things. A little savor of that time was with him when he came to the field of ruined coral. Below him was a trail of hacked and severed creatures, bare soiled sand and broken rock. His light struck a rainbow. Following it with his beam, he saw that the rainbow was rising in a broad column toward the surface. For some reason, the prismatic column was crowded with fish. There were more than he had seen so far: parrotfish, wrasse, tangs and, in great numbers, angelfish. For some reason the fish were circling, remaining within the colored circumference. He turned the beam down and saw that the numbers of fish increased with depth. Paddling away from the destroyed terrace, he followed the rainbow down.

So many fish, he thought, lovely in their numbers. A cloud of angels — and on the edge of vision the trembling barracudas, waiting to pick off stragglers. Ten feet farther down the column and the track of destruction, his light fixed on the plane.

Its serial number was stenciled in black on the blue-gray skin. Hoping to keep clear of debris, Michael moved away from the face of the wall and descended from open water. The beam of his light was just large enough for him to get a working picture of the wreck. The plane was upside down at a forty-five-degree angle, nose foremost into the reef. The rainbow column rising from it was composed of the last dregs and fumes from its fuel tanks. Somehow they had failed to discover a slick on the surface. The cabin door on the side facing Michael was open, showing the empty passenger seat just inside. The seat next to the vacant one had something piled on it, something obscured by the swarms of fish of every shape and species that teemed in it. Through its open door the cabin looked like an aquarium tank — but not an aquarium, he thought, swimming over with the light. More like a fish market's display bin because of the sheer volume of the creatures. No responsible scientific or educational enterprise, no aquarium, would confine living creatures in such insufferable density. He closed on the upended aircraft and poked his light into the cabin.

Of course the remains of the pilot were inside, and of course the fish were there in uncountable numbers to eat them. The remains were hugely swollen, stuffed into khaki cloth, and the head was so horrible that it frightened Michael into dropping his flashlight, leaving him traumatized in sudden darkness. He had to hurry down after the tumbling illumination while its beam careened over the coral wall, lighting crevices where half-coiled morays darted, lighting pillars of sea snow, the tiny flakes ceaselessly falling. A barracuda, drawn by the light's filament, made a lightning charge. He finally managed to get a grip on the handle about ten feet below the plane.

He wrapped the light's strap around his wrist and began to explore the space behind the seats. His hands were trembling, his entire body was. He worked hard to avoid looking at the dead pilot; the corpse was a revelation, an undeniable demonstration of the ghastliness inherent in material existence. The swelling was unbelievable, the beard and hair grotesque, also the lipless teeth. The whole vocabulary of features made a distinctly different statement.

Creatures had occupied the large storage space behind the seats and they fled his light in a scurry of fin and claw. He used his hands very tentatively, exploring the inside, hoping to keep his fingers intact. There had been dive mittens at the shop but he had chosen canvas gardening gloves instead. He had been down on enough wrecks to know that without a securing line he had better not venture too much of himself inside. Doors could shut forever. The aircraft's position was unstable; the whole thing could shift and plunge off the reef and into the Puerto Rico Trench. The trench began about three miles away, all of it dark and all of it down.

He could see the two cases and a tubular package that might contain paintings. He leaned as far forward as he could to get a hold of one of the cases but the tanks on his back stiffened his reach. At last he caught a piece of one with the light. Just as he did, he felt the plane he was leaning on begin to shift. For a moment he thought he was imagining it. Then he pulled out, trying not to fuck it up in the rush, trying not to spring his own deathtrap. When he was out he thought again he had imagined it, the shifting. No way to be sure.

Finally, swatting at shadows, feeling himself buried alive, half unconscious with fear, he got the tube. He held it for a moment between his legs and its weight bore him down;

he had to inflate the BC slightly to hang on. Next he got one of the cases into the seat beside the pilot. The swarming fish made him shudder with loathing. With both cases and the big tube he began to consider how to get all three of the things to the surface. He was breathing hard; all at once it struck him that he had not once checked his pressure gauge. When he did, he saw the arrow trembling on the edge of the red zone. He had been overbreathing like a rookie. The sight of it put ice in his blood.

Easy, easy, he said, speaking to the fish, to the pilot, his pal and fellow aquanaut. He gathered the cases and started up.

He had ascended about ten feet by his wrist depth gauge when he began to feel the straps of his BC contract. Everything he wore, all the gear, weight belt, tanks, seemed to be squeezing him sick. Allowed a tiny window, a glimpse of calm, he tried to run through the diver's mental checklist. As the straps gripped him, he saw the BC ballooning. He had gone down with too much air in the thing and it had contracted under the water's pressure. Now as he rose it expanded, and as the binding cut into his flesh, his speed of ascent went out of control.

Don't breathe! Don't breathe was the thing, the only thing, because a single intake of breath would do to his lungs what air was doing to the orange BC — puff them out like a kiddie's birthday party balloon until, like one of those merry little numbers, they popped, blood and tissue splattering his chest cavity. The higher he rose the more unbearably pressed the weight against his thumping, stifling heart, feeling like Cousin Clarence in the malmsey, the pain it was to drown, right, and the dreadful sights of water and the men that fishes gnawed upon. He tried exhaling the little swallow of soiled used air he was holding inside. The rule of ascent was follow your bubbles — no faster. Follow the bouncing ball. But the bubbles he could bring to the party were few and small, and he rose faster than they. The kids would be disappointed.

Then the air in his tank ran out. He did not trouble to waste the priceless energy required to reach the J-valve. Moreover, he had no free hand. He was clutching the shit he had gathered in the plane like life itself. And of course there was no need for air — au contraire.

The surface faintly lit with lovely moonlight was up there, a dream, a distant notion. But now he was in the real world, the water one, and he was drowning like all the others. One with the million million water bozos, blue bathing beauties, Phoenician sailors and narcotrafficking *pilotos,* all the other airless losers beneath the undulating sparkle of the briny deep. Fear illuminated him, lit him up. The loss of heaven and the pains of hell. The crushing pain, unbearable, the bindings slicing off his arms and legs. In his personal eternity he waited, waited for air, and he was dead, for it was not forthcoming. He dropped one of the cases and saw it spin down out of sight.

Then suddenly, in one violent moment it was all different. But it was not death, it was light, it was air. He saw the dim cabin lights of the dive boat and the huddled shadows of the men aboard it. Unawares, he inflated the swelling BC and ripped the regulator away from his drowned face.

When he breathed there was nothing. No relief, no air. How was it possible? He was on the surface. He had broached, it seemed to him, like a Polaris missile. His addled consciousness bore a moment of memory in which he looked down on the dive boat from the cruising altitude of a hot-air balloon, the killer balloon he had ridden to the surface. He took another famished lungful. *Nada, rien.* A heart attack, he thought. Or some drowner's dream. On the third try he knew he was breathing, the old plant back in motion. But he had come up too fast.

So he waited next for the agony, the bends, an embolism. It turned out he was fine, more or less. He floated, holding his two recovered packages like rescued babes. Roger was shouting at him over the sound of the water against the hull, shouts that were hoarse whispers. Hippolyte was beside him in the dark. He knew perfectly well who they were. He raised his mask to his forehead and breathed to his heart's content. Eventually he was able to speak.

"I'm not going down there again," he told them.

17

T HERE WAS SOME unpleasantness over the lost case
but eventually they headed back to the landing of
the Purcell house.

"It goes down to eight miles, Roger. It's gone."

When they were halfway back Michael asked him what
was in the cases.

"*Objets d'art.* Artifacts for sale. In fact," Roger said,
"they were already purchased, which is why I'm upset."

"I really am sorry, Roger. It's a miracle I was able to get
the two of them."

"Our customers are not pious. They may not be grateful."

Michael wondered briefly how their ingratitude affected
him, but he did not ask any more questions. Nor did he
ask any questions about Lara. He had followed her to the
ranks of death; that was where his encounter with the late
pilot had placed him. On that ocean, he thought, in that
darkness he had no friends.

Finally Hippolyte took Michael back to the dive shop.

Roger had debarked at the Purcell house landing. Hippolyte, young and inexperienced at docking, made something of a commotion at the dive pier. The two small children he had left in the shop were still there, asleep. Hippolyte stayed long enough to help Michael out of his wetsuit and check the compressors. Then he took his toddlers by the hand and disappeared into the night.

Michael walked the distance to the hotel in a kind of despair. More than anything he wanted to be with Lara. At the same time he felt that he had lost her. She had betrayed him into a different world than the one they were meant to share.

Coming up the back stairs he ran into Liz McKie, the journalist.

"Where were you, Michael? Were you out on the reef?"

"Are you kidding?"

"I heard a boat." She put a presuming hand beside his ear. "You look wet."

He moved his head away. "I . . . was in the water. Just on an impulse."

"You don't say."

"I've been hearing drums all night," Michael said.

"We've had a lot of drums for sure. It's the *retirer* for John-Paul Purcell. They're marking that at the lodge. Didn't Lara tell you that?"

"She did say something about it."

"Did she tell you about the lodge?"

"I don't know anything about the lodge. I've never been there."

She stared at him, eager and confused. Her eyes were wide with excitement and fear. "Hey, Michael, tell me. What's going on, buddy?"

"I don't know. Really."

He wanted very much to ask her whether she was afraid of the story she was trying to write and the people she was trying to write about. He let it go.

She smiled as though she were sorry for him and went away. There were soldiers milling around the patio of the hotel when he got there. No one was in attendance at the desk. A couple of the soldiers were passing a bottle of four-star rum, making a halfhearted effort to sneak it.

Having no one to provide him a destination, he went into his room without turning on the light and lay down on the bed. The rhythm of the drums had changed but there still seemed to be four, pursuing one another's beat, never stopping. The ocean he could see through the window gave no promise of morning.

18

T HE TEMPLE, the *hounfor* where Lara danced, was
constructed of leaves and branches, leaning against
the Masonic lodge. In its center, running from the
earth floor to the roof, was the twisting, snake-shaped pole,
the *poto mitan.* Around it Lara and about twenty *serviteurs*
connected with the Purcell family were dancing the ceremony of reclamation for Lara's brother.

They faced a leaf-and-branch wall all inset with niches
where bottles were stored. The painted bottles were decorated with glitter and worked with spines of tin. These *govi*
contained souls, some those of the living, others souls of
the dead. The bright, thick-fleshed leaves reflected the firelight.

The drums beat without stopping for John-Paul, each
one enclosing its own spirit: ogan of iron and brass, and
maman, petite, rouler, seconde. Four fires burned around
the *poto mitan,* which enclosed the celestial serpent,
Dambala. The songs called on Papa Legba, the *loa* of the
crossroads, and on Baron Samedi, the *loa* of the dead. The

drums played all night and Lara had been dancing most of the night with them.

From time to time, the *mambo* offered her more rum and brought the sacramental cloth, adorned with a *vever* of the god. The wall of painted glass where she danced was heaped with blossoms — different flowers for different forces, thorned bougainvillea and sour apple for the forces of *bizango* that John-Paul had served. Then frangipani, poinciana, loblolly pitch apple and myrtle. Different blossoms stood for *rada,* others for *petro.* For Marinette, flowering geiger. Above all, Lara was hoping and dreading that Marinette would come.

"John-Paul," she prayed, "if you are back from the sea, if you are safe from Guinee, make Marinette give back my soul."

From inside the lodge building someone shouted at her. It was a woman called Hilda, who was waiting inside with two Colombian *milicianos*. Lara walked out of the firelight into the half-darkness around the lodge. Hilda took Lara by the shoulders.

"You look stoned, little girl," the woman said.

Lara looked away. The woman pursued her, trying to keep and hold her eye.

"It was good, eh? I hope El Trip told you what happens to you if you try and cheat us. See if your spooks can help you."

One of the *milicianos* said something in Spanish. Until then he had been repeating *"Hay que matarlos,"* urging no quarter.

"Trip has a soft spot for you," Hilda said to Lara. "He thinks you went to bed with El Caballo." She meant Castro. "Is it true? Did he give you an emerald? Did you fuck that son of a whore?"

"Everything happened so fast," Lara said.

She went back; no one stopped her. The drums kept their beat, the fires were burning down. She began to dance again as the first light broke over the Morne. As she danced, she saw Roger Hyde walking on the edge of the airstrip with one of his servant boys. The boy was carrying two cases, one in each hand. One was a rectangular steel trunk, the other was the metal cylinder into which she had put the family's island art collection.

On his way to the lodge, Roger called to her.

She shook her head, and he spoke to the people with her in Creole, asking them if she was in a trance, mounted. They answered excitedly, all speaking at once. Not yet. Not yet, they all said, but it would come soon.

The *mambo* gave her a slug of raw rum and took one herself and pressed the inlaid banner cloth of Erzule against Lara's sweating forehead. Then she covered Lara's face with it, half suffocating her in rum and perfume that was as raw as the rum. A god, Ghede, told a comic story about stealing the perfume with *bizango* guile. Everyone clapped for the god, who tipped his tall hat. Everyone was laughing. It was a woman using the voice of an old man. He or she pretended to describe Guinee. Baron Samedi. Baron Kriminel.

Lara kept dancing although she was not under the god's power. She was looking for her brother's spirit in the drum and for her own. The *mambo* followed her dancing moves like a midwife. Another old woman danced the parody, the mimicry of a midwife. She laughed. "Doupkla," she said to Roger. "Marassa. Twins!"

"*Merde,*" Roger said angrily, which made the *mambo* laugh heartily.

Some Colombian *milicianos* came out with lights. More

and more the Colombians had been using their own people for security, preferring not to rely on the locals. The *milicianos* ordered Lara and Roger inside the lodge. Lara tried to keep dancing but Roger took her hard by the hand and led her in.

"It's all right, kid," he said. He released her and took a swallow from a bottle of Barbancourt that stood on a table.

"Why is it all right?" Hilda asked. "I see two cases there. I want three."

The guards reacted like mechanical soldiers. They jammed their magazines forward, looked over their shoulders, spun around their leveled weapons.

"Hay que matarlos!" one said. He disliked *negros* and fancy *blanquitas.*

"What is this, Rogerdodger?" Hilda asked. "Que fuckerando?"

"We had her friend make the dive. That we recovered anything at all was" — he stopped for a word and smiled very slightly — "a miracle."

Lara watched the pretty little woman stalk Roger. Her fine Botoxed countenance was suddenly transformed, reduced to a face that was simian and rabid with greed. Or with an imitation of it, a pretend greed more frightening than the real thing. Roger, very frightened, kept his cool. Lara moved to stand beside him.

Roger put the cases on a mahogany table in the meeting room, took out his keys and opened them.

Hilda settled down, went to her briefcase and removed what looked like an order pad.

The first case was divided into drawers, and the drawers contained emeralds. Some of the sections had cut emer-

alds backed with lined index cards that listed each stone's
weight and variety. Some drawers contained loose stones,
apparently uncut.

The second, cylindrical case was jammed with matted,
soaked sheets, jelled into a single mass by the seawater that
had penetrated the tube.

"So," Hilda asked Roger, *"que pasa?"*

"It was hers," Roger told Hilda, shaking water from the
tube. "Mostly watercolors." He reached in and took the
sodden cylinder partway out of the case. "And a few can-
vases. Island work."

"It was mine," Lara said. "And John-Paul's."

Hilda looked at her without speaking.

"Well," she said finally, "that's nice, huh? Art. I like
that."

Outside, the brass and iron ogan pulled the *rada* drums
behind it. The rhythm of it was irresistible. A man
screamed in a woman's voice. Lara tried to part the edges
of her drawings, half listening now for her brother's voice.

"Well, guys," Hilda said, "the one you say you lost is the
one we needed to move. This is a tragedy."

"I take the responsibility," Roger said.

Hilda observed him.

"You fuckin' straight about that. No offense."

"I figured I had to get it out of here before the Americans
and their friends took over," Roger said. "They already run
the capital. It was a risk."

Hilda wiggled as though she were shaking off his argu-
ments.

"Hilda, Lara's friend Michael almost lost his life retriev-
ing this."

"That's great, Roger. But you, me and him" — she put a

hand on one of the *milicianos* — "we are responsible also. You know what I'm saying?"

"I'll make it up," Roger said. "We'll make it up between us."

"What if the shit turns up in Miami?"

It seemed to Lara that Roger was getting his confidence back.

"It isn't going to turn up anywhere, Hilda. It's well and truly deep-sixed. I was right over him."

"What if the guy moved it? Maybe he's down getting it now."

"They'll be combing the bottom, Hilda. Raising the plane. Any hour."

Everyone fell silent. One of the dancers came to the sanctuary window and held up a placard for them to see. It was a red heart with a black star at its center. He moved it to the rhythm of the drums.

"Where is this diver? Who is he anyway, this Michael?" Hilda said. "Why didn't he come here?"

"He didn't come, Hilda, because he's just a friend of Lara's. He's a professor, her boyfriend. He knows nothing about us. He doesn't want to. And the less he knows, the better."

"He's scared to come," Hilda said.

"Wouldn't you be?" Lara asked her.

The man with the starred heart kept moving the placard in front of them as if it were a signal, a sign of something about to happen. But the drums only beat on.

"Let him come here," Hilda said. "Let him tell me about it."

"Hilda," Roger said, "if we were stealing from you, do you think we'd go to all this trouble to deceive you? The plane is down. If we'd left it there, you'd be out everything."

The man with the star and heart began to tap on the window to get their attention.

"Who the fuck is he?" Hilda screamed. *A miliciano* waved him away.

"He's Ghede," Lara said. "He's the god."

After a moment Hilda said, "Tell him to come. This Michael. Tell him come here and look at me and say he lost my property."

Roger looked at Lara and then said, "He won't. Would you?" He looked down at his watch. "Look, you have to leave. The Americans, their police, will be coming out here."

"You hope," Hilda said. "No, man. Send for him. I want him to tell me how it was."

Everyone looked at Lara.

"All right," Lara said. She took a roulette table chip out of her pocket and gave it to Roger. "He'll come for this."

"You see how it goes, Roger," Hilda said. "The more we talk, the more we get back from this dead airplane. Now I want to meet your diver."

Roger looked at the chip. "Hilda, we'd give you the pilot if we could. The plane too. Unfortunately that's not possible."

"Do the best you can," Hilda said.

At the window outside, Ghede danced for them.

19

MICHAEL MANAGED to get to bed before dawn. He was almost asleep when morning lit the slats of his room, a breeze stirred the netting around his bed. The birds of day were chattering, a rattle of bad pennies that gathered force in the space where the drums had been. When he listened closely enough he found the drums still there, faded into sounds of dawn but relentless. Out on the ocean, a great mass of cloud was approaching, armored and crenelated, triumphally white. Before its fortress front, if you looked with the right eyes, with Lara's eyes, it was possible to see the powers of the island withdraw into dark green groves, into their own reflection under the surface of Guinee below.

He had waited for morning; now he was jittery in the light of day, the barred half-light of his room. While he sat naked on the bed with his head in his hands, a knock came. Certainly expected, he thought. He put on his pants and opened the door to a tall, bony boy in white jeans, Dolphins cap reversed. The boy handed him a table chip, number oo, two ovals of leaf green, the action chip from the Caribe Hilton . . . the night before? The night before that? Before that? What have I won?

With the island sense of drama the boy waited, not so much for a reward, Michael thought, as to watch his reaction. In any case, his errand was not over.

"Lady says come on back."

"What have I won?" Michael asked.

"Says you be comin' on back. Come on back. Everybody says. They be angry wit you."

The 36 chip was in his trousers pocket and it occurred to him to hand it to the boy to take to Lara. The holy number trumps. Emeralds out of luck.

He put the second chip in his pocket and asked the boy to wait for him and closed the door. When he finished dressing and went out he found the reporter McKie at his door. The boy Lara sent had moved off. There were strangers about. There were white men, and more government soldiers.

"You were diving last night," McKie said softly. As though she affected to admire him and as though that were a trick.

He shook his head.

"Did you get the goods?"

"C'mon," he said as he might in grade school to a girl teasing him. This riled her. She looked around to see who heard. Michael wondered where the boy with the chip had gone.

"Let me tell you something, diver. This is Iran Contra Junior. This is senatorial aides, huge right-wing connections, the whole Argentina colonels' lobby, and it's linked to the death of Allende and it's linked to coke. And your girlfriend — she *is* your girlfriend, is she not? — your girl-friend's family's activities in this island? Got it?"

"My word!" Michael said mockingly. "Goodness me! Holy shit!"

"You're a fucking fool," she said. "Fucking fool you are. You're involved in contraband and conspiracy. You'll sit in an island jail — you want to talk blood on the walls? Want to see the ants eat it? And then you'll do federal time — if the *milicianos* don't feed you to their spider monkeys."

"Was there an accident?"

"My dear shithead! Pretty shithead! I have the story. I will set you the fuck free if you talk to me. I have the story and we will walk away together with it. The feds will not let you walk. The island will not let you walk. The *milicianos* will most certainly not let you walk."

Two white men, Americans, approached, one of them walking much more rapidly than was customary here, in the heat of the day.

"OK," said Miss McKie, "one is the Drug Enforcement dude from the capital. The other is the consul up here. You don't have to talk to the DEA guy if you talk to me."

"What about your boyfriend?" Michael asked.

"Who?" Shocked! "Who, Junot?"

The American consul acted scornful and grossly over-qualified, a savant of many climes, wasted here. Too wasted even to put out a hand. His name was Scofield. He was waspish toward McKie and never addressed the DEA man, whose name was Wallace. Michael deduced that they had not met before the preceding few hours.

"Tell them what you do, Michael," Miss McKie said.

Michael told the Americans he taught English at Fort Sa-lines. They had never heard of it. Wallace treated him like an apprehended criminal and they walked down toward the water.

"So who's in the plane?" Wallace asked. "An American citizen?"

"I really don't know," Michael said.

His tone seemed offensive to Wallace. For a moment Michael thought he would get some kind of epicene mimicry for his impertinence. *I really don't know.* Cop sarcasm to show him his place.

"No? Maybe you know *what's* in it."

Michael waited for someone to mention the dive shop but no one did. Turning onto the Carenage toward the harbor, they passed the youth who had brought Michael the roulette chip. He stood at the edge of a gathering crowd and knitted his brows. Jeeps full of island soldiery passed.

Consul Scofield led them to a waiting boat of the island Coast Patrol. Beside it, he drew himself up in a political manner and introduced himself formally.

"On the advice of Vice Consul Wallace, I've asked the American citizens to come down to the harbor. Obviously there's been a tragedy — a plane is missing and we have some eyewitness reports of an explosion occurring the night before last. On such short notice we haven't been able to do much, although we have located what we think is the scene of an accident. Vice Consul Wallace would like a few of you to come out while we try to raise the remains."

"I'll go!" Liz McKie said, raising her hand to volunteer. Wallace and Scofield looked at each other. Scofield shrugged.

"We'd like Mr. Ahearn to come with us," Wallace said. "Especially we'd like Mr. Ahearn. We think he might be able to help us."

Michael tried to understand what the DEA man might mean by this. As far as he could remember, he had not damaged the plane in getting the doors open or left any particular evidence. No one had raised any question of a dive except McKie, who was keeping her own confidence.

"I don't understand why I should have to go out there," Michael said.

"Don't you?" Wallace asked. "We think it would be helpful if you were there. Maybe as a witness when we bring up the body. We think it would be really helpful."

"Actually," Consul Scofield said, "it would be real cooperation. We'd be grateful. Bureaucratic reasons."

"It's psywar," Liz McKie said quietly to Michael. "He wants you out there because he wants you scared."

"Should I go?" Michael asked.

"He might give you local problems if you don't."

"You might help me with those."

"It's possible. It's also possible he might get smart and go have a look at the dive shop. "You *were* down there last night, no?"

Michael looked away without answering and they set out, beyond the small pretty harbor to the edge of the reef, or at least to an arm of it, one that stretched from the base of the Morne that towered over them to the Puerto Rico Trench, eight miles of descending terraces that bottomed out in the deepest spot in the Atlantic, pole to pole. It was toward that spot that the plane's third case was little by little making its inexorable way. At least Michael hoped it was.

On the way out Consul Scofield remonstrated with the hot-rodding Coast Patrol helmsman.

"*Doucement,*" he called over the engine noise. "*Doucement, mon ami.*"

The man at the wheel laughed agreeably and did slow down a bit. Wallace kept his eyes on Michael, who was balanced on a small partition in the stern beside Liz McKie. He was holding the green roulette chip in his hand.

"Where'd you get that?" asked the insatiable McKie. "Souvenir or something?"

Michael shrugged.

At the edge of the reef, where the plane had gone down, a single barge with a rusted A-frame crane was riding the rising surf. Steersmen held their boats against the incoming tide.

Coast Patrol divers had lowered and secured the crane's light tackle. As the Americans' boat came up, a young man on the barge, an islander, supervised the operation. There were two divers in the water, who looked to be *blancs*. The man in charge signaled to the crane operator.

"He's done this sort of thing before," McKie said to Michael. "He's got a pretty good idea what's down there."

Michael, who knew, took a deep breath. The crane started up. Everyone waited for the surfacing.

After a minute or so, the pale blue water swirled and clouded. A lubricant can hit the surface. One of the hands on the barge began to shout in Creole. Michael thought he could make out a shadow on the deeper side of the reef line. He shielded his eyes from the declining sun.

Then some kind of creature raced to the surface only a few feet from his boat. It was a huge unwieldy thing, crazily shaped but certainly, Michael thought, alive. It had antennae, claws, spines, a tail. And it was surrounded by fish, fish of such variety and in such uncountable numbers that anyone arguing that the fish were gone, that the reef was barren and lifeless, would stand refuted. Tangs and butterfly fish and wrasses. And there were shrimp adhering to the main body of the creature, hanging on.

Then it hit the surface, and Michael thought that the size of it was the strangest thing. Nothing that lived on the bottom, nothing he could think of, was of such a size. Nothing went surrounded by fish in such a way, in the mandibles of shrimp, wrapped in some kind of rainbow jelly.

The surface did not at first hold it down. Whatever it was showed most of its length to the breathing world, then spun. In their boats, the barge hands and the *blancs* and the others watched it spin across the top of the water. The thing bounced along the surface as though it were trying to escape a predator, zigzagging, darting this way and that. It made a noise that was like the farting of a hundred exhausted penny balloons.

On the barge, one of the deck hands called out in Creole and everyone turned to him. He called a second time, repeating the same word. The man at the wheel of Michael's boat took off his gold-braided cap.

"What is it?" the diplomat asked.

"It's a floater," said Mr. Wallace.

Then Michael realized that the rainbow jelly was oil slick, that the fish and other creatures were eating the creature. He caught a fraction of a second's whiff of foul breeze. It had a kind of face, Michael saw, a head and body. Both were beyond imagining. They bounced like enormous corks in the sandy water over the reef. They were the remains of the pilot, of whose posthumous existence Michael thought he had seen enough. He turned away. Then he noticed that even hardboiled Mr. Wallace had found another quarter on which to cast his cop's gaze. The islanders crossed themselves — and Michael too — in recognition that Guinee awaited plenty of those who served the trade. Fishermen and emigrants, smugglers and divers, pilots and contrabandists and policemen, all might find their way to Guinee one day, at the bottom of the trench at the bottom of the world. Even for Miss McKie, who was just passing through for the world's information, especially for Miss McKie, Guinee yawned. Even Miss McKie uttered a prayer.

20

WHEN WHAT HAD BEEN the pilot was decently encased and removed to the Mennonite Hospital, Vice Consul Wallace led everyone back to the hotel. He was eager to get in touch with Colonel Junot of the new National Defense Forces.

"There is going to be a police investigation," he explained to everyone. "We'd appreciate it if folks would make themselves available to the authorities."

The consul, Scofield, seemed mainly interested in his ride back to the capital.

"Where's Colonel Junot?" Michael asked Liz McKie. From the inshore patio of the hotel, he had just caught sight of the young man Lara had sent him in the morning.

"I have no idea," she said. "Contrary to what everybody thinks, Colonel Junot and I are not joined at the hip."

Michael stood up. The consul and vice consul, who appeared to have little to say to each other, were observing him from another table.

"I'm off," Michael said.

"What?" McKie said. "Where?"

"Maybe I'll get some sleep."

The American consul came over and greeted Liz McKie facetiously. She treated him in the same spirit.

"I'm sure you'll want to get back to the capital by daylight, Consul. Better see that the police give you an escort.

"Since the coup," she explained to Michael, "there are burning roadblocks. They call 'em 'Père Lebrun,' and they're what 'necklaces' are in South Africa. You can ask old Van Dreele. Some of the locals aren't too impressed by diplomatic plates. Some of them don't care for the good old Stars and Stripes."

"I was going to ask you about that," the consul said. "I thought you might have seen Colonel Junot."

McKie sighed. Shortly a car was provided for the consul.

"Are you a friend of Lara Purcell?" he asked Michael as he left.

"Yes," Michael said, without much thinking about it.

"Give her my very best," Consul Scofield said. "Tell her she's missed. She's the most fascinating person on the island."

"I'll tell her."

On the way upstairs, Michael signaled to the boy from the lodge that he was coming, and went into his room. Before he could slide the lock, McKie pushed her way in and was standing next to him.

"Oh my God," she said, "you're going after her."

He began wearily to deny it.

"Bullshit. You went down to the plane. Did you get everything?" She had no need of an answer. "That chip — that's from her, right? You're going back to her."

Michael began to throw a few things in his shoulder bag.

"You don't get it, do you, Professor? These Colombian militia types are without mercy. They kill *everyone*. Do you think they'll clear out of here and let you live? Do you think that smart bitch will give you a break? Even if they let *her* live?"

"I don't know about the Colombians. They're buying the hotel. Maybe they'll see reason."

She stood in the doorway and put a hand against the door to block his way.

"Reason!" She screamed the foolish word at him. "Why can you not see the deep shit you're in? Wallace will get you. He'll work you into an indictment of this whole business."

"You've told me about the stick," Michael said, zipping the bag. "Tell me about the carrot."

She seemed to calm down a little.

"The carrot, Michael? The carrot is you give everything you have about this operation and its political connections. Not to mention its academic connections. I get you off this rock. We get you lawyers. We get you immunity." She paused, out of offers, trying to think of treasures untold beyond immunity. "Didn't you see that pilot?" she asked. "Don't you think death is kind of ugly?"

"What are you, Liz, a philosopher?"

She stepped aside.

"You're so nuts," she said. "My story is a public service."

Outside, the boy from the lodge was still waiting for him.

21

THEY WENT ALONG the road in one of the hotel's old four-wheel-drive sightseeing vehicles. The thing was in grave disrepair but serviceable. Finally the boy, whose name was Christian, drove them down a dog-leg. At the end of it they got out and started walking in the direction of the ocean.

Stunted pine, mahogany and schefflera grew around them; in spite of the fresh runoffs the soil was dry. When they had gone something like a mile over the trail they came to a gate with razor wire, framed by tall walnut trees. There was hardly any breeze.

Men in camouflage fatigues approached them. Michael saw that they were not islanders but lean mestizos, apparently the Colombians of whom he had been hearing so much. They looked in his shoulder bag; one looked at his passport.

Christian spoke to them in fluent Spanish, telling them, as far as Michael could understand, that someone — he, Michael — was on the way through. A few minutes later they came to a cleared field, an airstrip with a hangar and what might be sleeping quarters. Somewhere, someone was beating the ogan, the iron drum of the ceremonies. People were singing.

"*Wete mo danba dlo,*" Christian told him.

They walked on. Goats munched on the shaved cane and the coarse grass between the dismembered stalks. Once in a while one raised its head and turned a wise, wicked gaze on them.

At the far end of the strip, people were sitting in the late-afternoon shade, huddled around the Haitian-style houses and the strange churchly bulk of the lodge with its columns and tower. Another drum picked up the beat of the ogan.

He was trying to keep up with Christian when he heard a high-pitched cry, almost a scream. He looked across the cut canefield and saw Lara running toward him. She was waving a red handkerchief over her head.

He stopped and waited for her. She came calling his name. Two Colombian *milicianos* rose as though to intercept her, but finally made no move. She took him by the hand and led him down the road to the lodge building and the *hounfor*.

"I'm with my brother," Lara said. He put an arm around her shoulder. She seemed crazy and lost.

"You see, Michael," she said, the words spilling out as they walked toward the *hounfor*. "I'm with John-Paul again. We'll be together."

People came out of the thatched buildings where they had been sheltering to look at them.

"Come, Michael," Lara said. "This is the ceremony of *retirer! Wete mo danba dlo!* For John-Paul." She was holding his arm with a grip that hurt. "Michael, he came to me. Back from Guinee, from the bottom of the ocean. But I have to wait for Marinette because she has custody of my soul."

Her hair was streaked and soiled with ashes and straw and insects, living and dead.

"Yes, my love," he said.

"And, Michael, you have a soul, eh? You have a *petit bon ange*."

"Is that what it's called?"

"That's how we call it," she said. "And it's here," she said, "it's here for you."

Gently Michael moved her past the crowd of people in front of the lodge and through its entrance. There might once have been doors; now there were only cool shadows that closed around them. In the meeting room of the lodge he saw Roger Hyde together with a middle-aged woman and a pair of *milicianos*. The woman looked out of place there. She was dressed for the city and did not have the appearance of a believer.

"I admire your coming, Michael," Roger Hyde said. "You did the right thing."

Michael thought there was more force of conviction to the first statement than to the second.

"What a nice-lookin' guy," Hilda said. "Anybody tell you you should be in the movies?"

"Nobody," Michael said. The *milicianos* watched Hilda.

"So sit down," Hilda said to Michael. "Like dry off. Maybe you still wet, huh?"

"No," Michael said.

"I'm just joking with you. What's your name? Michael? I'm just joking with you, Michael."

"No," Michael said. "I had time for a shower and everything. To get the salt off."

"To get the salt off," Hilda repeated. "Was there blood?

The guy didn't have, like, blood all over him? From the impact?"

While Michael tried to stammer an answer, the drums and the *hounfor* outside exploded in triumphant rolls. Lara had disappeared from his side. In a moment he heard her outside.

"She's calling the name of the god," Roger told him.

"Such a pretty girl," Hilda said. "Pretty girl, pretty fella. Nice pair you make, the two of you."

"I thought that *immediately*," Roger Hyde said. "As soon as I saw them together."

"So what happened, Michael?" Hilda asked. "What were you doing out there with our airplane?" She laughed as though the situation were droll. "All in the dark and wet there. What happened?"

"It was easier than I expected," he said. "It didn't take much —"

"What were you doing out there, Michael?" she shouted, interrupting him, pushing her powdered slum-kid's face in his way. "Who told you to go down?"

"Lara did," he said. Saying it that way made him feel somehow like a snitch.

"Lara did," Hilda repeated. "How did you find out the plane was down?"

"She told me. She came to the hotel."

"She came to your hotel and asked you to dive on a crashed plane? And you said sure?"

"I was ready to do it."

Hilda looked him over.

"Love, huh? Love makes you do crazy things, right?"

He nodded.

Hilda asked one of her Colombian *miliciano* associates if

he thought love made people do crazy things. The soldier considered a moment.

"*Claro que sí,*" he said.

"Sure it does," Hilda confirmed. "Lie and cheat and steal. All that. Right, Michael?"

"The first two containers weren't a problem. Maybe I got careless." A certain tension settled on the room. Roger Hyde drew himself up and looked at the floor. Hilda grew more serious.

"Careless," she said and shook her head. Michael understood that he should not be accusing himself of things. "Careless is bad, Michael."

"But I don't really think I was careless. I handled everything step by step."

He could see Roger cheer up a bit. He felt fairly calm.

"My friends say," Hilda told him, "that when somebody makes a mistake, somebody's got to pay. It goes for you. It goes for me."

"He did his best," Roger said. "I saw him chasing down after it. It got away from him in the current. Anyway," he said, refilling a glass of brown rum, "we can make it up. We can cover it in a few months' business."

"Other people have made mistakes," Hilda said.

"Everybody does," Roger agreed.

"But," she said, "you don't want to hear about what happened to them." Then she laughed and said something in Spanish that made the Colombians laugh loudly and caused Roger to warily chuckle.

"So you did your best, mister? If there was a next time maybe you'd get it right?"

"I was careful," Michael said. "I did my best. I went after it."

His plea had a summary quality that made him uneasy.

"I should carry the cross?" Hilda asked. "I should explain for you characters? Get my own ass in the bad chair?"

"It can be made up," Roger said.

"I," Michael said, "I'd do anything I could to make it up."

"Yeah?" Hilda asked. "There in America you would?"

"Yes," Michael said.

"You're fucking right you would. If you thought you could just go back up there and forget about us you'd be making a bad fucking mistake. If we called on you, you'd deliver."

"Yes," Michael said.

"You know," Hilda said, "I'm not like the *cabrones* that say America this and America that. I lived in America a long time. I lived in Rhode Island. Americans are sometimes OK with me. Some of them." She looked from Roger to Michael, a guilty comic coquette's glance. "The good-looking ones, know what I mean?"

"These two are good kids," Roger said. "John-Paul loved them dearly."

"Go on," Hilda said, "go ahead, Michael. Dance the dance there. Go with your friend."

When they were outside, among the drums and the exhausted *serviteurs,* it struck him that Hilda and her friends must be waiting for night — that whatever happened to them would happen shortly. The darkness came down quickly, the sudden night of that latitude. Lara whispered in his ear.

"Marinette! Marinette is here."

That was as much as she could tell him. Hours ago, seconds before, she had fallen. After falling she had no idea of

time; she had fallen into the darkness at the world's first beginning where the only light came from the glowing snake.

"Where is my brother?" she had asked.

She was with him. She saw Marinette in the snake-light.

"John-Paul?"

"Little sister," said John-Paul.

She felt great sadness and cried. She carried the two *govi*
that held their two souls to the wall of the *hounfor*. Michael
was beside her.

"Lara," he asked, "what do you think they'll do? Are
they going to let us go?"

But she was past such questions, dancing now with an
old woman in stained silk and lace who held a lit cigar in
her mouth. The dance was a whirl, and as the old woman
performed its turns, she made a noise between her clenched
teeth. The noise sounded like the rage of a child, but it
was a louder and more savage sound than any child could
make. Her eyes were not dull like those of the other dancers, but keen and charged with an anger as fierce as her
scream. Lara, trying to imitate her, to match her moves, in
her own exhausted state could not get close.

The old woman, or man, whichever it was, took the cigar out of her mouth and flicked the ash like a comedian.
She threw back her head and screamed louder. What
followed might have been composed of words or mere
sounds, he had no way of knowing. Instinctively he moved
away.

"Marinette!" Lara shouted.

Then Marinette seemed to find Michael and to laugh at
him. She pointed and screamed and then planed out her
arms in imitation wings and circled Michael as though she
were pretending to be an insect. Lara was laughing.

Marinette embraced him; he stood stock-still, choked by

the smell of her sweat-drenched silk and lavender perfume. There was a gray wig on her head, a painted beauty spot on her cheekbone. Her clothes seemed genuinely old, taken out of a chest, and her with them, out of the same chest or the same grave. He followed her gestures and saw that she was holding a pair of rusted gardening shears. She swung the shears over his head, screaming into his face. Lara was screaming too, kneeling. The other *serviteurs* pressed around her, holding red cloths to her head, kerchiefs and bandanas. Then Marinette swung out of sight, into the darkness.

Michael knelt and brought Lara to her feet. She had stopped screaming. She rested her head against his shoulder. He thought she looked more beautiful than he had ever seen her.

All at once a plane passed overhead. From its lights, he thought it was a medium-sized passenger plane, a DC-7. It flew at an altitude that seemed to him no more than a few hundred feet. Looking after its passage, Michael saw that more *milicianos* had gathered at the edge of the lighted *hounfor*. There were a dozen or so, looking easy, rifles slung. It seemed to him that there were more islanders as well, swaying to the quiet drumming that had followed the departure of Marinette, clapping their hands gently. Lara clung to him. The *mambo,* smiling, gave her some of the colorless rum to drink. Lara put the stuff away like water. When Michael tried the bottle, he gagged on less than a mouthful.

He tried to take Lara in his arms, to comfort her. Give her a moment's rest. Somehow she had the soiled-rag smell about her. He looked into her face and saw that he was holding Marinette. She laughed at him, her eyes were sly, bright with triumph. She began to scream, a kind of yodeling ululation, in mockery of him. She spat and he saw her hatred. She waved the shears in front of his face.

"Lara," he said.

Someone shouted in Creole.

"Kiss the blades," someone said evenly.

He tried. He would think afterward that he had tried. He could not close his eyes on the hateful stinking figure that whirled in front of him.

"Hag," he said. He screamed it. People shouted. He began to fall; by the time he righted himself, he saw Lara again. She had turned away from him.

"Lara!"

It was Lara, no longer Marinette. It was his Lara, he thought, returned to him, beautiful and wise, her legs steady beneath her, her moves that of the athlete he remembered. She carried two of the small decorated jars that stood on shelves along the temple wall. She turned, facing him across the *hounfor.*

He thought he heard shots in the dark forest around them, in the direction of the ocean. But now a tall man stood in front of him, a man in a bent stovepipe hat. He wore an old frock coat and red vest decorated with knitted *vevers.*

"Michael," Lara said to him. "This is Ghede. See what he has for you." The *serviteurs* came to Michael as they had to Lara, pressing their red bandanas and kerchiefs against his head. He heard the drums beat. "This is for you, Michael," Lara said.

Then he wondered if she was the same Lara after all.

In front of him was the tall man in the top hat, smiling.

"Michael," Ghede said. "Michael. Mickey boy."

"He's Ghede, Michael," the *mambo* said, offering him rum.

"Drink it, Michael, mate," said Ghede. Then he was gone.

Listening, Michael knew immediately the drums were speaking to him. It was so obvious, he thought; they had been playing out his fortunes from the first moment he had heard them, so many hours before. They had never left him. They were filled with fragments of his life's time, encoding voices he knew. In the rhythm of the *seconde* he could hear his own breathing against the respirator, as it must have sounded under the ocean.

"Oh, Michael," Lara said. "Our Ghede. Papa Ghede. Our great Baron. Baron Samedi."

He wondered if he had ever realized how sweet her voice was, how strange and lovely were the little touches of island music in her speech. He looked at her beside him. Whatever love meant, he thought, was here.

Now Baron Samedi came again, out of the darkness, around the *poto mitan* where the spirit of Dambala held power. Baron Samedi pushed a wheelbarrow. The wheelbarrow had a rivet that made it look flexible. In it, its red strangled tongue brighter than anything else in the flames, was a goat.

"Hi ho, Michael," said Baron Samedi. "Hey, look here what I have got for you."

He began to back away. Lara went with him, after him. The *mambo* came, and the great Baron, the Baron Samedi.

"Who are you, for Christ's sake?" Michael asked. He was backing away fast, moving so quickly that Lara had begun to hurry to keep up with him. "Who the fuck can you possibly be?"

Baron Samedi began to laugh, a false hearty laugh like a clown's or a clergyman's. He shook the wheelbarrow and the goat in it. The drums beat for them.

"When the man has his life between living and dying he got to know me. Ho ho. Such a rogue, Michael. Don't know what lies between."

"And it's where he's at," Lara said. Or someone using Lara's voice, because she would never say "where he's at."

"Hey, Michael," Baron Samedi called. "Live for Sunday or go to the graveyard. What for Michael — am I Baron Samedi?"

"Listen to him, Michael," Lara called. She sounded some distance away. There were fewer fires. The crowd was milling close.

"Yes, I say!" shouted Baron Samedi. "I am the Baron Samedi. Without Friday, I can't be. Without Sunday, ain't no me. In that space . . ." and the Baron drew a long breath, pronouncing a word that Michael was not born to hear.

"Who are you, man?" Michael asked him.

For an answer he got clown laughter and ho ho ho and the shaking of the wheelbarrow. Suddenly he was at close quarters with Roger Hyde.

"If I were you," Roger said, "I wouldn't try to play these games."

"What?"

"If I were you," Roger said, "I should save my life."

When he ran into the darkness, the drums seemed to be keeping after him. He was running before he knew it, himself taken by surprise. He had started somehow, and thereafter it had been impossible to stop, impossible to do anything but increase speed. Waist-high scrub kept tripping him up, throwing him against the stony ground and stripping his skin as though he were being dragged the distance he covered. Then he was running in shallow water with a firm rocky bottom. He saw fires ahead and turned to get his bearings. He had covered a great distance from the lodge. Its ceremonial fires were still burning and he could see figures outlined against them.

The drums sounded on, and it was still his time they beat. He ran through black space, splashing, running as it were in his own grave, running away from Baron Samedi, whose dark space he inhabited, the presiding god of his life and lord of his adventures. The lord of all who had made a grave of their lives. Baron Samedi's drums still beat for him.

But there were fires ahead too, and electric light flickering among them. He was encouraged, although the water around his legs was growing deeper and the bottom grew softer and clung to his steps. He heard shots, someone was firing; the reports were mostly single but now and then there came a burst of automatic fire. None of the shooting was close as far as he could tell.

His exhaustion made a copper taste in his mouth. He could hear his own breathing, a dry wheeze, unrelieved. Still gagging on the taste of the fiery alcohol, he wanted water. He put down a hand as he ran, trying to scoop up something cool and drinkable; the move threw him off balance, into a series of crazy-legged staggers from which he recovered with difficulty. His cupped hand brought up something bad-smelling, much too thick to drink and too repellent.

He thought he heard other runners behind him, splashing through the same stream he had followed, fanned out from bank to bank. He saw a car maneuvering along a road fifty yards away, halfway up a rise. The fires ahead were close to the road, barrel fires that stank of gasoline and sent out fumes of oily black smoke, visible in the fire's own light. The hill along which the road ran was walled by ridges of congealed earth whose contours showed against the firelight like the definitions on a relief map. At the top of the same hill, searchlights were being played around the valley. He did not try to stay out of their way, only to find his own by their intermittent patterns.

For a while, as he ran, he believed absolutely that Baron Samedi was running with him, not staggering in the same ungainly manner but moving along beside him, for amusement, to exercise his possession. He had to concentrate to put the thought out of his mind.

Reaching the road, he saw that its surface showed the traces of paving. For the first time since he had started running he was confronted with his own rational intentions. He had been running with the god entirely. The god had been his pursuer, his goal, the notion of his nearly mindless flight, the process of running.

Along that remnant of a modern road he felt he was either leaving the illusion of his master's presence or entering an illusion in which he was free of it. He had stopped running. There was no more breath for it.

Before him was a *blocu*. Fifty or so island people, almost all of them men, stood in the road. Piles of old half-burnt tires were heaped along the shoulder. Big hundred-gallon drums filled with tire strips sent up a black stink, like meat butchered and roasted raw, the living flesh of some vile animal. Farther from the road he could see stripped tires piled in towers and burning. Others stood as though pre-

pared for the next occasion, a midnight Mass of Père
Lebrun, when the living meat would be less exotic, a more
familiar dish, and the mystic ritual would be transubstanti-
ation in reverse as every grain of life transcendent was
burned howling out of the beast.

A big young cane cutter approached. "Hey mon, you got
somefin' for me, yah?" "*Lajan, blan,*" another kid called.
Patois hung at that end of the island. Her part. Who? Lara,
her name was Lara. Her soul had belonged to Marinette, as
his to Ghede, the Baron Samedi. There was a race and he
had run it. She was gone.

He had wads of dollars and local bills. He straightened
them out, flexed them with an appealing snap and delivered. He half shouldered his way through the crowd, a discreet, polite and most accommodating way of shouldering.
The handouts worked somewhat; by the time he was out of
bills he was among the losers and runts who had been
forced to the rear and had nothing to play against his fear
except their need and desperation. These were not to be de-
spised, because he had survived the *blocu.* There had not
been much tourism on the island for years, and the hatred
of the islanders had cooled somewhat.

Walking beside the potholed road, he was never alone.
The drums kept him company. Figures passed him, some
moving so quickly he might have been standing still. From
the darkness people shouted his name. Voices addressed
him as Legba; sometimes he thought he was wearing a
stovepipe hat. On his chin he felt the fringes of a false
beard.

There was a car behind him sounding its horn. He
moved farther off the road, but after the car had eased past
it stopped for him. It was a Mercedes, the sleek fender cov-

ered in red dust. An island soldier was driving it and there was a soldier with an automatic rifle beside him.

The rear door opened and Michael saw a long-legged olive-skinned man with a neat mustache settled in the back seat. He was in uniform; his collar was adorned with the red tabs of a senior British officer. It was Colonel Junot, the administrator of the new order, graduate of Fort Benning and veteran of Grenada.

"Spare yourself, Ahearn," the colonel said. "I'll take you where you're going. Oh me," he said, seeing Michael's spattered trousers.

"No," Michael said. "I've worked it out."

The colonel reached out patiently and took him by the arm. "Yes, yes, worked it out, very good. Here, come take a ride with me."

So Michael got in and the soldier handed him a *Miami Herald.*

"To sit on," the colonel explained. They followed the road along the Morne until they were driving far above the ocean, with the stars overhead and a risen moon at the edge of the sea's dark horizon. Low clouds dissipated against the jutting rocks below the road.

"Too bad, you can only get the view here by daylight, Ahearn. This is one of the great views of the Western Hemisphere. The French wanted to fight the Battle of the Saints here. On that bay!" He pointed into darkness to the right. "Well, you can't see it now."

When they had gone a little farther, Colonel Junot said, "Dutch Point! Lovely peninsula. I suppose you know we haven't been having many visitors recently. It's our somewhat violent political situation. Social unrest, you see."

"Yes," Michael said.

"Well, here's a secret. The cruise line companies use Dutch Point all the same. They just don't tell their passengers where they are. They tell them it's Point Paradise. Where could be sweeter? Mum and Dad and the wee bairns go to Point Paradise, wot? So close the bloody roads to the point, and put a skirmish line of about a hundred-fifty rent-a-cops to seal it off. Let a couple of colorfully garbed vendors and a steel band through. Good, isn't it?"

"It's good thinking."

"Yes," Junot said, "good thinking on the part of the cruise lines. Paradise Point. Bloody tourists disport themselves in the surf, no idea they're in between a Glock and a griddle, I mean a *hot spot*. No, they're in *Paradise*. If we had those rent-a-cops stand down, the bastards would think they'd died and gone to hell. They'd experience some social tension."

"You're taking over, aren't you, Colonel?"

The colonel shrugged modestly.

"Will you continue the Paradise Point tradition? With the cruise lines?"

"Certainly," the colonel said. "But one day we won't have to build paradise with rent-a-cops. With luck — and, unfortunately, a little discreet repression — we'll have good old paradise back all over the island. Paradise, paradise! Upscale, upscale!" The colonel laughed and sighed.

"I'm afraid for my friend," Michael said. "Lara Purcell. I left her behind. I'm afraid they may hurt her."

"I know your story, Mr. Ahearn. I know you're a thoughtful man, friend of herself. Well, you don't have to worry. Because everything is under control, including the lodge. And she will be safe, I can promise you. So you don't have to worry. Understand?"

Michael said nothing.

"How'd you like to live in someone else's paradise?" the colonel asked.

"I can't imagine it."

"Think of it as a misfortune. A huge fucking pink misfortune."

"I guess I don't understand," Michael said. "I haven't been here long."

"Yah, man. But I think you understand, eh? I would be surprised if you don't have a piece of the picture."

The road headed down toward a concentration of light at what appeared to be the end of the island. The mass of land gave way to an expanse of rolling moonlit ocean; just short of the waves were fields outlined in geometric patterns of red and white light.

"We don't have a choice, do we?" the colonel said. "We've inherited bloody paradise and now we've got to live by selling it. Paradise and every naughty little thing." He leaned back in the seat and slapped Michael on the knee.

"Oh yes, we have all those naughty things they want and don't need. The drugs, the coffee, the chocolate, the rum and the orange-flavored booze, the tobacco, the girls and the boys. Shouldn't have them. Bad for you. Live longer without them but they're oh so nice, yes, indeed. How you want them all. And that's our fortune."

The car passed a checkpoint at the approach to the All Saints Bay international airport. There were soldiers everywhere in the uniform of the island's new army. The soldiers took a look inside the Mercedes and waved them through.

"Hands across the sea, right!" Colonel Junot declared.

"You get to Washington, say hello to my friends. Tell them I want my medal from the President! Soldier in the war on drugs!"

The car stopped and the driver came around to let Michael out. He stepped out of the air conditioning and into the warm ocean breeze.

"Soldier in the war on ganja. Soldier in the war on cocaine. That's right! Soldier in the war on sugar and sweeties. And the war on rum. The war on cee-gars. The war on fancy jewelry. The war on screwing and gambling and general do-badness. You tell the President that the armies of Paradise salute his tall fine figure and the war on everything is going great. Tell him I knew his daddy and I want my medal."

Michael had only the shoulder bag he had taken from his hotel room. He moved among the watchful soldiers toward the wooden terminal. Beside it, a DC-7 stood with its engines running, attended by half a platoon of American Special Forces soldiery in green berets. He went into the harsh fluorescent light of the terminal building. The young Cuban American woman at the commuter airline's desk checked his ticket. There was a mirror in the wall behind her desk and he could see that he did not resemble Ghede. But the Baron was waiting for him at the Emigration window, where a customs official was flanked by supportive soldiers. The Emigration man was Baron Samedi.

"You got to have your pink form," Baron Samedi said. "Otherwise you can't fly."

Michael checked his pockets twice. He checked them again. He searched his shoulder bag several times. He could not find his pink form.

"For God's sake," he told Baron Samedi.

"They got no special rules for you, mon," the Baron said. "Either you give me your pink form or get out of line. There are people behind you."

Michael turned and saw that there were indeed people waiting to pass Emigration.

"I flew into Rodney. I don't think they ever gave me the thing," Michael said. "I've got to get on that plane." In fact it was absolutely the only thing on his mind and he was ready to kill, or to die, in the process of boarding it.

He was at the point of losing control when he saw Colonel Junot enter the terminal. The colonel saw him and came to the window.

"Pass this man," the colonel said. "This is my messenger."

Baron Samedi had departed from the customs officer, who mildly stepped aside. It had been a farewell message, a little game typical of Ghede.

Colonel Junot had come into the unadorned departure lounge with Michael. Shaking hands, he quickly turned aside.

"Uh-oh," he told Michael. "I see someone I don't wish to meet." He hurried out through the customs gate where he had come in.

Making his way to the last bench in the departure area, Michael saw Liz McKie standing beside the ladies' room. She looked extremely angry. Two island soldiers were with her. The soldiers by contrast looked happy and well entertained.

McKie saw Michael and called to him.

"Jesus Christ! What are you doing here?" she demanded.

"I guess I'm leaving."

"You guess you're leaving?" She stared at him for a moment and then said, "Watch this stuff." She was surrounded by computers, cameras and recorders, all packed away in cloth, Velcro-banded cases. "I have to go to the john and I'm not leaving my stuff with these bozos."

"We're insulted," one of the soldiers said, laughing at her. "We don't steal."

"That's right," the other one said. "We never steal from a friend of Colonel Junot."

"Where is Colonel Junot?" the first soldier asked. "Not coming to see you go?"

"Fuck you," McKie told the soldiers. "Watch that stuff like it cast a spell on you," she told Michael. "Don't let these characters near it."

"We have to come in the lavatory with you, miss," the first soldier said. "Orders!"

Before she could react, they were doubled up with laughter, dapping.

"I mean," Liz said to Michael, "keep an eye on it."

While Liz McKie was inside, the soldiers tried to decide whether to pretend to steal some of the equipment, drawing Michael into their game. In the end — probably, he thought, because he looked so disheveled and unhinged — they let it pass.

When she returned to her possessions, Michael wandered out to the veranda of the departure lounge, which was the only place to get fresh air. It was a restricted area but the sentry there let him out. He took in the wind of the island and of the ocean, the jasmine and burning husks, a touch of the rubber stench. From ever so far away — although it could only have been a few miles — he heard the drums. He tried to understand whether it was his life he heard beating there, and if it was his life, his heart, where it might be inclining. But the drumming was only itself, only the moment. In the flickering lights beyond the airport fence, he thought he saw the wheelbarrow, the tongue of the goat.

They boarded the plane and Michael saw that one of the Special Forces soldiers was a woman, bespectacled, pretty, with man-sized shoulders.

When Liz McKie tried to address the woman soldier, the soldier stared straight ahead and addressed her as "ma'am."

"Ma'am yourself, troop," Liz McKie said to her.

To further McKie's humiliation, she was seated just behind and across the aisle from Michael on the flight to Puerto Rico. The impulse to explain it all was too much for her and she had not added up the emotional tokens yet.

"I cannot believe this," she told him. "I mean, it's all so typical I can't believe it."

She had been *persona non*-ed out.

"I mean, not with paper, not to the State Department, but my ass is flung out. I mean, my friend — my friend, my lover." People stopped their own conversations to hear her.

"I mean, this is your U.S. Third World hype — screwing of the classic type, right. So there's corruption. And some right-wing official Americans are in on it, right, and their Argentine, Chilean colonel friends, the worst *cabrones,* but hey, that's cool. It's cool because they're rogue elements, they're not really us. Us are the good guys, us are the girl Green Berets, and we fix everything and we throw the bad guys out. Except we don't quite get the bad guys out and the good guys turn out to be not very different from the bad guys and, hey, it's all looking kind of the same as it was.

And when you look, the rogue elements are gone, vanished, except not quite. And some idiot reporter buys into the good guys' scenario and what happens to her? I mean, I knew it! You know when I knew it? When I saw you! I thought, Who the fuck? And I knew things were screwed."

"Sorry," Michael said.

"And my friend Junot, your friend . . ." She shook her head, out of words for it all. "And that woman."

"Lara."

"Her."

Without whom, he realized all at once, he would live a life suspended on the quivering air, the beat of loss, moment by moment.

When they were coming down at San Juan, McKie spoke to him again.

"So maybe you got rich, huh? Maybe you'd like to talk about it?"

"No," Michael said.

"I saw the drums got to you," Liz said. "I know about that. Did you find God?"

"No," he told her. "It was the same, understand? What happened to you happened to me."

She shook her head, looked at her watch and began to cry.

22

ROOMS WITH BATH were available at the Student Union during the summer. Michael Ahearn rented one. Every day he used the pool at the athletic department. Often he swam hour after hour, amazing and finally unsettling the young lifeguards. After his swim he would go to his office and read himself to sleep in a chair.

Some floors of the Union building contained dorms. When term started in late August, the leaden quiet of the place exploded in adolescent riot. Sometimes, in the dead of night, the screams would make him think he was on the island again. The place he was afraid to name, even in his thoughts.

Arriving home the previous spring, he had immediately sensed Kristin's simmering anger. After three days of empty politeness she found the boarding passes for their flight to Puerto Rico, his and Lara's.

Then she permitted herself rage. In Paul's hearing, she said things to Michael he would not have imagined her saying. Her passion was startling, even to him. Crouching like an assassin, she delivered calculated, scalding, phosphorescent anger. It hurt to the depths of him.

"Conniving son of a bitch," she said. "You do not maintain a mistress on me, fella. Maybe your pals will think you're a sport. But I don't think you're a sport, I think you're weak."

She went on and he had nothing to deploy but grief. He had had time to realize what he had done to Lara. What he had done to Kristin seemed not nearly so bad but she seized it like a whip and beat him lame.

"Do you think I came to you with no dreams of my own? That all I wanted to do was plant roses? But finally I gave you everything. And everything involved you. Oh yes, I thought you were hot shit, fucker! I thought you were the beginning and end and nobody really knew how great you were but me."

"I wanted more," he said.

"Oh yes," she said. "Maybe you think I don't understand such desires? But I had a life to complete here. Our work and our child. And I thought when we got that taken care of — with a little luck — life would provide. And we would learn the trick of getting more. You and me. That was a key thing, ya? Us."

She put a wad of paper towel under the kitchen faucet and wiped her face.

"I thought, wait, it will come. Then you humiliate me with that creepy greasy whore. The Latin bombshell."

"We can come through," Michael said. "We can put it behind us."

"Not," she went on, "that I wasn't hearing reports. Not that I didn't have suspicions. But I chose not to see any of it."

"It was a passing madness," Michael said. "Insanity."

"Passing?"

"Yes, Kristin. That's over, over."

"Well, it doesn't matter," she said. "I'm seeing to my own survival. Mine and my son's."

He had another flash of the fever that had burned him on the trip. It seemed never to quite disappear. Confusion came with it, a touch of panic.

"Look, Kristin, I know you can understand this. The thing came. There I was. A crazy impulse. Fugue."

"Chance of a lifetime, right?" she said. "I understand. Understanding's not enough. Confess and be understood? Be absolved? No dice."

She backed away from him, fixed him with her dead father's eye.

"You see," she said, "my vanity is not the problem. Respect. Respect is the problem."

She was silent for a while.

"I feel strong now somehow. I feel I see clearly. I don't want to let you talk me out of that."

"I'll never leave you again," he said. Dumb thing to say. It earned him her slight scornful smile.

"You know the secrets of the heart, Michael. I know you do."

"Don't forget it," he said, trying to turn a joke.

"But you talk too much," she told him. "My father was right about that."

"God," he said. "That old sod rat."

She laughed.

"But you *do* know the secrets of the heart. You truly do. Me," she said, "I look for signs. I ponder signs."

They stood around the kitchen not speaking. He watched her, hoping for forgiveness, feeling like a sick dog.

"I never questioned your loyalty," she said. "I feel so insulted." She looked distractedly out the window.

When she walked out, the first astonishing blaze of the fever struck him. A bolt of raw heat. His wrists twisted and swelled so that he could not hold up his hands.

And that was how it ended. There was nothing for him to do except leave. Paul hid from him that day. Before the week was out she had a lawyer.

The next day he had simply moved into the Student Union and he was still there when the term opened. The night sounds there worked themselves into his dreams, which were nearly always frightening and febrile. Breakbone fever dreams.

The symptoms grew worse; he had not been in the Union a week before he landed in the hospital with what appeared to be dengue. There were uncertain factors. One of the doctors thought it might be a kind of malaria. His case was a very bad one, with cerebral complications, and for a few days his vision failed. Half blinded, he was alone in a bright gray maze, buried alive with his pain and his visions. He kept trying to straighten himself out around the drums but they brought him only confusion.

He had the sensation of being wrapped in dry rubber, along with thirst, fever and unreasonable pain that made him think of Père Lebrun. They put a wall of sheets around his bed. Within that was the wall in which he was buried, blind. He was trying to find Lara. Lara was trying to find him.

Kristin came to see him while he was in the hospital. There was no mistaking her tall soldierly form.

"Anything I can do, I will do," she told him. But when he left the hospital it was to return to the Union.

The doctors told him that it was likely he would suffer a relapsing fever. They gave him a supply of pills and told him to avoid alcohol.

Phyllis Strom had passed along to the larger academic world and every few days he wrote a letter of recommendation for her, trying his best not to let it slide into boilerplate. His new teaching assistant had come from Russia as a child. She was plain, intelligent and efficient. Lately he had been subject to lapses of memory and the young woman did her best to remind him of what had to be remembered. She attended his classes too, insisting they were sheer delight to her. Ahearn had never before doubted his own authority in a classroom. Everyone said he was witty and incisive. That fall he felt less sure of himself.

All summer he had been waiting for the consequences of his adventure to strike. Sometimes he worked himself into paroxysms of anxiety over everything that had happened, unable to eat or sleep or read. At other times he was passive and numb, untouched by fear or remorse. The details of the trip slipped away from him. He forgot names and sequences of events. Eventually his sense of unreality about the time in St. Trinity overcame his dread. Nothing happened to concern him personally. He had no communications, none of any kind, from Lara. For a long time he heard nothing at all from Liz McKie.

He grew close to Elizabeth, his Russian-born TA. There was no question of romance. Growing up in the provinces like a Chekhov heroine, Elizabeth had come to realize that she and her parents commanded a cultural level beyond that of the Americans they lived among. The transplantation had destroyed her father. All through her years of education she had sought mentors, individual Americans more cultivated than the rest. She had had a favorite high school teacher. Family responsibilities compelled her to settle for college at Fort Salines and she was making the best of it. Attracted by his erudition and despair, she had settled on Ahearn as a guide for the next stage of her enlightenment. They drank tea with lemon in his office at odd hours.

"Your memory problems are from the fever," she told him one night. "You should see a doctor."

Ahearn, as usual, agreed.

"You're young," Elizabeth said. "You must act somehow."

He laughed. "And you're old beyond your years, Elizabeth. Wise beyond them."

"You're a valuable man. Truly!" she said. "You are exceptional. The beauty that you have absorbed, the poetry and wisdom. I hope," she said, "you don't think I'm flattering you. I'm speaking out of turn, I know."

"Oh, I can tell," he said. "You're flattering me for a grade."

"May I say something more outrageous?"

"Of course, Elizabeth."

"Your wife is foolish to leave you for that man. Cevic."

"She knows what she's doing. I have my problems."

"Excuse me," said Elizabeth. "But to say this is so . . ." He watched her avoid the obvious in three languages. "So unfair to yourself." She watched him slyly. "What is the worst problem?"

"Oh," he said. "That I have no soul."

One night in the mall he had a strange encounter with Paul. It was dusk, a wild gusty night. Paul was skateboarding with three friends; he and his father nearly collided at the sloping edge of a parking lot.

"Whoa," the boy said. Every time Ahearn saw his son he was surprised at the boy's growth, the thin arms hanging from wide bony shoulders, the long legs and hardening jaw. Paul skated around him in what felt like a hostile enveloping motion.

"Well, how are you?" Ahearn said. The fact was that they had seen very little of each other over the summer and fall. Partly it was because of his illness, but Paul was avoiding him. Out of some self-mutilating impulse Michael had been allowing it. Also, he realized, it was a way of punishing Kristin. The three boys with Paul backed away, withdrawing from a parental encounter.

"Hey, I'm like OK," Paul said. His face began to change. In a few seconds a startling range of expressions showed themselves. Ahearn thought it was like the approach of a *loa* to the possessed.

"Yeah, I'm OK. How are you, man?"

"Don't call me man," Ahearn said.

"Oh yeah, sorry," Paul said.

"We'll go hunting this year," Ahearn said.

The boy kicked his board and went off in something like terror. His friends fell in behind him.

Finally he had a note from McKie.

"Check this out!" the note said. Enclosed was a clipping from the "News of the Americas" column in the *Miami Herald*. It announced that Marie-Claire Purcell had been appointed the island republic of St. Trinity's ambassador to France. There was a small picture of Lara.

Ahearn rarely shopped for groceries. He took his meals at a Greek diner called, for some reason, the New York Restaurant. Occasionally, out of some old homing habit he would find himself walking the aisles of the local

Albertson's supermarket. The place was a state of mind, its light peculiar. People picked their way along in some engineered commercial condition, watchful, grim, passing each other with secret glances. Some of its charge was erotic, and he was aware that men who knew how it was done could pick up women there.

One day, prowling Albertson's, Ahearn saw Kristin and Norman Cevic shopping together. Norman pushed the cart and Kristin scanned the racks, ready to strike, seeking out specials, twofers, coupons. Ahearn moved closer to the wall, hiding. He put his glasses on to watch Kristin's diligent gathering. It seemed to him he knew her every motion from the inside out. It was impossible for him to believe he would not go home with her.

They were very affectionate together. Cevic, Ahearn thought, looked younger. His bearishness was subdued. Kristin looked at peace. Shopping. On their way to the register, Cevic put his hand across the seat of Kristen's jeans. As Michael knew she would, without saying anything, without turning to him, she moved his hand away. Michael foresaw her reaction as precisely as he knew the feel of that warm denim. Before taking hold of his hand with hers she pressed it against her behind for a moment, for the fraction of a second. So it appeared to Michael.

He watched them at the cashier's line, joking about the tabloid headlines, both of them with wallets out. Cevic managed to keep his hands on her. It occurred to Michael that he himself had nothing to lose. He was driven and it might be *petro,* he thought, the *loa* that drove him. He could easily be on them before they got to her car. He would kill them both with his bare hands.

The next day he went to the doctor and asked for sleeping pills and tranquilizers.

"What do you want them for?" asked the impolite young doctor.

"Social self-discipline," Michael said.

The doctor gave him a long look but he got his tablets.

Deer season opened. The bare trees of Fort Salines were hung with carcasses. Men and women in DayGlo were everywhere. On impulse, he called Alvin Mahoney. He had seen Mahoney only twice since the beginning of term. Both times Alvin had been in a hurry to take himself elsewhere. He had actually acted offended over something, although that was quite impossible. It was only awkwardness and shyness. The maladroit Mahoney.

"Alvin! Mike!"

"Oh jeez," said Mahoney.

"What do you mean, oh jeez, Alvin?"

Alvin tried to laugh politely.

"Thought we might have a shot at the critters," Ahearn said to him. "What do you think?"

"Oh jeez." Then silence. And then he said, "You know my back is seizing up something fierce. I ain't . . . you know."

"Ain't you, Alvin?" He had no idea why he had called the poor man. Perversity. "Well, I promised my boy I'd take him this time."

"Paul?"

"Paul," Ahearn said. "My son."

"Oh. Sure."

Truly the man was a trial.

"Alvin, do you mind if I borrow a couple of your pieces for tomorrow? The twelve-gauges, maybe."

"Well, I only got two. You wanna borrow both of them?"

"Yes, I would. If I may. If that's all right."

Alvin could hardly refuse, although it was close.

Hardly anyone glanced at him twice as he walked the shotguns in and out of the Student Union, the barrels poking through a crushed cardboard box. That evening he called Kristin. It was Monday evening of the second week of the season.

"Look, you didn't say a word about this," she told him. "He isn't prepared to go. He hasn't the junior permit. You must be joking."

"I'll tell you what," Ahearn said. "I'll come by in the morning and ask him if he wants to go."

"Have you lost your mind, Michael? I mean, really! No fucking way is he going hunting with you. You should —" she began, then stopped herself.

"Right," he said. "I should have taken him last year."

He started drinking, straight Scotch, about two in the morning, watching a seventies movie with the sound off. The film made him think about how ugly and stupid the seventies had been. Bad luck to have spent his youth in them. After a couple of hours he took some gear and his shotgun and drove out to what had been his house. He left the guns in the car.

It was still dark when he arrived. He rang the front doorbell and knocked on the door. Stepping back, he saw upstairs lights go on. Fucking outrage, he thought. His house.

Inside, Kristin and Norman Cevic were screaming at each other. The light went out, the front door swung open. In the light from the door he could see Norman crouched on the stairs.

"Get the fuck out of here, Michael. You get the fuck out of here. I called the police. I have a gun and so has Kristin." He did seem to have one, across the knees of his pajama bottoms. What Michael could see of him was fearsome: he was bare-chested, hairy, altogether enraged.

"Great Scott," said Michael. "Kristin too? What about Paul?"

Kristin and Cevic tried to shout each other down again.

"You crazy fuck!" Cevic shouted at Michael. "You stupid drunken asshole. I'm gonna kill you if you don't piss off."

"Well," Michael said, "that would just be murder, buddy, because I don't have a gun. I mean, I have a shotgun in the car but I'm not out here waving a gun around."

"Dad?"

Paul was standing at the corner of the house, visible in the porch light. He was wearing a Vikings jacket over pajamas. Both Cevic and his mother were shouting his name.

"Hey, Paul," Michael said. "I thought you might want to go hunting. I mean, it's kind of improvised, the time and so on. You remember I mentioned it."

"Yeah," Paul said. "But I don't really want to. I might another time."

"Right," Michael said. "You remember last year? We were talking about . . . What was it? The religious aspects of hunting. The ethical dimension."

"Right," Paul said. "Dominion and stuff."

Kristin came to the front door and looked at him. He stared at her for a moment and turned to his son.

"Say, Paul," he said. "Come and kiss me."

Paul looked to his mother and then came forward and kissed Michael deliberately on the cheek. The boy he had taught that there was a right way of doing everything, and he was trying to be careful not to do it wrong.

"My blessing isn't worth anything," Michael said to

him, "but you have it." He spoke to Kristin in the front doorway.

"I don't suppose you want to kiss me?"

"No," she said. "The cops are coming."

"That's a good reason," Michael said. "How about your boyfriend. Hey Norman," he called softly. "Want to kiss me?"

"He doesn't want to kiss you," she said. A little runic *Gioconda* smile there. "Go home and go to bed."

Christ, she's smiling, Michael thought. What a hardass. But when he looked again he saw her eyes were full of tears. Maybe a moment's forgiveness, a new love maybe stoking the ashes of the old. He thought of Erzule's power. Anything was possible.

Let's go upstairs to bed, kid. He thought he should say that to her. But he did not say it. Officer Vandervliet had arrived. The young cop climbed out and stood in the welter of light spun by his own blue and red patrol beams. He bore himself with the caution appropriate to domestic dispute calls.

"Hey, Professor Ahearn! Hey, Miz Ahearn!" Michael saw that Kristin was still in the doorway. "Hey, Professor Ahearn, put your gun down on the road."

"I don't have a gun," Michael said. "It's in my car."

"Nobody got a gun here?"

They let him see for himself. Michael thought with some satisfaction of Cevic crouched in the darkness like a sniper, trying to move his shotgun out of the shadows.

"Well now," said Vandervliet, "we were told there was a gun on the scene."

Vandervliet wanted to talk about it. Michael obliged him, letting the lusty couple return to their quarrelsome bed. In a few minutes he was able to demonstrate that no crime had been committed.

"Thought you had an old dog out here," the cop said. "Didn'ja?"

"Gone," Michael said, "that dog."

Under the gray bones of a mackerel sky, he drove west in the direction of the wooded swamp where he had hunted the year before. The day grew cold and it was windy. A few icy flakes rattled against his windshield but there was no snow on the ground as there had been then. Fields of dead corn, the stalks butchered to stumps, bent to the weather. A few miles on he passed Ehrlich's wholesome *bierstube*. Half a dozen pickups had already gathered outside it with carcasses to display. A sign on the roof of the place promised music that evening.

In the next county, there were hardscrabble fields broken up by glacial rock and stands of poplar. Derelict barns sagged into the long grass. Every other mile a trailer stood half hidden in the scrubby woods, exposed to the road this time of year by the trees' bare limbs. A few of the trailers showed smoke at their chimney pipes. Most had one or two beat-up old cars beside them.

When he reached the Hunter's Supper Club, he turned into its lot and parked his car beside a brand-new Lincoln Blackwood. The Blackwood was quite a spectacle, with its brushed aluminum sides and fake exotic wood. It looked enormous and expensive among the heaps in front of the Hunter's. Lined up with it were a battered Buick Century, a Sierra, a couple of Harleys.

The bar of the Hunter's was darker than he had remembered it, more of a refuge from the wide cold sky outside. Ahearn forgot his annoyance with the vehicle outside. He was looking for Megan, the barmaid. He asked the old man behind the bar about her.

"She been sick," the old man said.

"I'm sorry to hear that."

"You a friend of hers?"

"I used to come by, deer season."

The old man, who had watery eyes the color of Megan's, looked at him without fellowship.

"Season got her started on the wrong road."

"I used to get a bottle of Irish here," Ahearn said. "Willoughby's." He had no idea what the old man meant about the wrong road. "I wondered if you had it."

There were other customers. Two youngish couples at a rear table had turned to look drunkenly at Ahearn. He noticed a slight smell of stale marijuana from the booths.

For a moment the old bartender stood where he was, staring at them.

"I got to get it out," he said grumpily.

Michael glanced toward the bar, which the old man had left unattended. A woman in a wheelchair came forward out of the dark spaces in the back. She was thin and grinning. Her neck was supported in a brace that was part of the wheelchair. Her jeans and shirt were far too large.

The bartender came back with the whiskey and said, "This is Megan here. Hey Megan, you remember this guy here?"

What she tried to say might have meant anything. She could not look at him directly. Bending to shake her hand, Ahearn smelled tobacco and marijuana in her hair, along with other things. One of the middle-aged male customers came up without speaking and helped her wheel her chair away.

"Encephalitis, what it was," the bartender said. "Her there."

"I'm really sorry."

The old man leaned forward and looked slyly in the direction she had gone.

"Some say it wasn't that. Some say she went to the city and got a drug OD."

The sky was darkening, stormy blue-gray. He drove the two-lane through the battered fields for a while and then turned off on a dirt road. The road approached a tree line and he thought it must be heading for a creek. Instead it turned off to the left, and on the far side of a treeless rise, it intersected another road at right angles. The intersecting right angles were particularly sharp. Conforming to something, he thought, but who could say to what?

He pulled over and opened the bottle of whiskey. The liquor made him sweat in spite of the chill. He grew dizzy and leaned against the car window. He thought he might be hearing drums over the horizon. The fever swelled behind his eyes; he closed them.

He heard the sound of hoofbeats before he saw her. Coming up to him, she slowed the big black horse to a walk. She had on a padded jacket, breeches and a hard riding hat. She took the hat off and brushed back her long black hair. It had more strands of gray than he remembered. Her face was thinner, her cheekbones seemed more prominent, her skin a shade darker. Ahearn was struck by the size and fearsomeness of her mount. It was a jet-black gelding, wide-eyed . . .

"Your horse," he said, "looks like he eats meat."

"Island proverb," she said. "Big riders cannot ride little horses."

"Well," he said, "you know I'm ignorant of *les mystères*."

"Ignorant of *les mystères*." She mocked his accent. "But you're back safe and sound."

"And you," he said. "You too."

"I live in France now."

"I know."

"I was delivered. You could say God was good." Her horse seemed to bolt. She tightened the reins while it side-stepped to the soft shoulder of the road, righted itself and came back.

"Not to me."

She laughed at him. "Oh, Michael. But you betrayed me, eh?"

"You knew what I would do. You took me to hell."

She shook her head and then carefully dismounted. She kept short rein and touched his face with her free hand.

"Not at all. No, no."

"That was hell."

"My friend," she said. "That was the other thing altogether. You see it everywhere and that was it."

"The spirit goeth where it listeth? No thanks. It was the kingdom of hell. I'm still there."

She fished in the pocket of the padded khaki jacket and brought something out of it to show him. She had emeralds in her hand. Very big emeralds, it seemed to him, cut and shining even on this dark day.

"*Eh voilà!*" She held them in his face.

"Congratulations," he said. "Good for you."

"Don't you see, it's a sign. Don't you want one?" She thrust them at him. "Here, look, I'll give you half. Pick them out."

"No."

Exasperated, almost enraged, she put the stones away and got back in the saddle.

"Oh, my poor friend." The fierce horse was impatient. "What you wanted came to you."

"Came at me," he said.

"So, so, either way. Why did you ever think about it? So it came and you sold it out to save yourself. Thinking that you could."

"I don't want to think at all," Ahearn said.

"Because you were there, the mysteries opened themselves," Lara told him. "At your service until you hardened your heart."

"Were you Marinette?" he asked her. "Are you?"

"Only Lara again. Out of a bottle. As Marinette, if you had been less afraid I might have delivered you."

"It was hell," Michael said.

"Forget about it then," she said. "Don't bring such questions down on yourself. Or otherwise, learn to see clearer. Then maybe it will find you out."

"Maybe in a dream," he suggested.

"Maybe. Sure, because the questions are childish, aren't they?" Her horse stepped toward him. He moved back, out of the way. "The mysteries, the stories are for children. By the way," she asked, "how's your little boy you adore?"

"He's fine," Michael said.

"So," she said, "thank God, eh?"

He nodded.

"Courage, then," she said to him. Not mockingly but in a comradely or sisterly way. He stepped out of the crossroads to let her pass, and she rode on in the direction she had been heading. He could not imagine what could lie that way for her.

St. Trinity was conceived on a visit to Haiti with Madison Smartt Bell, the great chronicler of the Haitian Revolution. Enjoying Madison's companionship and guidance, I was able to share a number of adventures in Haiti which I passed on to the denizens of *Bay of Souls*. Along with him, I heard the drums and saw the fires at the crossroads.

He bears no responsibility for variations of the cult as practiced on my island of St. Trinity. The spirits lost in passage through *Bay of Souls* are entirely in search of their own light. They and I ask his blessing.

I also wish to worshipfully salute the memory of Maya Deren, beautiful and gallant rider to the stars, author of *Divine Horsemen*, which is the greatest of works on vodoun. Her insights will guide errant souls forever, all our lost brothers and sisters in pursuit of the light where the world began.

Action de grâce.

R.S.